HEAD AND TALES

Susan Price has been writing as long as she can remember. At fourteen she entered and won the *Daily Mirror* short story competition and at sixteen she wrote *The Devil's Piper*, a fantasy which was published just after she left school. Apart from writing, Susan has worked as a box-humper in a retail warehouse, a guide in the Open Air Black Country Museum and, for two days, as a dish-washer. 'As a dish-washer,' she says, 'I was a complete failure.' She lives in Tividale, in the West Midlands.

HEAD AND TALES

Susan Price

faber and faber
LONDON BOSTON

First published in 1993
by Faber and Faber Limited
3 Queen Square London WC1N 3AU
This paperback edition first published in 1995

Photoset by Parker Typesetting Service, Leicester
Printed in England by Clays Ltd, St Ives plc

A CIP record for this book is
available from the British Library

ISBN 0 571 17488 4

2 4 6 8 10 9 7 5 3 1

'Don't shake, Dad, don't shake,' the girl said. She squirmed on to the mattress beside him, put her arms around him and held him as tight as she could, thinking to hold him still, so his teeth wouldn't chatter and his breath wouldn't catch, and he could rest. But his shaking shook her too. His shirt was as wet as if he'd been standing in the rain, and he reeked sourly of old sweat, sharply of fresh sweat, and for all he shook as though with cold, he was as hot to hold as a dish filled with boiling stew.

She pulled away from him to look into his face, wondering if holding him made him feel better, or if he wanted her to let him go. But his eyes were closed, and he couldn't speak because he hadn't the breath while he was shaking. So she hugged him again, pressing her face sideways against his shoulder and tightening her arms around him as much as she could. It made her feel as if she was helping him.

They lay, the two of them, in one of the huts built for the navvies as they dug the canal, one of a village of huts, continually pulled down and built again a few miles further on, as the navvies followed their great ditch across the country. The walls were of wooden planks, the roof of oilcloth, and a low fire was the only light. The red-lit darkness held many stinks: fire-dried earth and fresh mud, the smell of meat fat, and beer, and the sour mustiness of a place where many unwashed men live. In a dark corner, where the firelight didn't reach, a small boy slept and snored on a damp bed of coats, shawls and bracken.

On the bed nearer the heat and light of the fire, the man went slack in the girl's arms, and began to breathe in longer, easier draws, with a sound like sighs of relief. His hair, long, dark, thick, and glimmering in the flame-light, spread over the dirty, lumpy pillow under his head. His beard was dark, but striped with grey at the corners of his mouth. 'Cold now,' he said, his voice scraping dryly, whispering, through his sore throat.

That was the way it went: first he was hot and shook; and then he stopped shaking and said he was icy cold, though he still felt hot to the touch. The girl let go of him, sat up, and reached for the mug of beer that stood near the fire, the red light of the flames coming and going over its crack-glaze surface. She brought the mug to him, and was alarmed at the effort he had to make to raise himself on one elbow. She watched his hand holding the mug, and saw it quaver from the weight – her father, Linnet, who could dig all day and carry her little brother on his shoulders when they tramped from one diggings to the next. He might die, she thought, and, fascinated with fear, her mind clung to thought and repeated it over and over: he might die, he might die, he might die . . .

He put the mug down and rolled on to his

back, lying flat, limp, exhausted. She got to her knees and covered him over with the damp, muddied blanket, and with the coats and shawls that friends had thrown over him before they'd gone off to the wedding, saying, 'Let him sweat it out.'

'Shoulda gone to the wedding,' came his grating whisper. From a distance, from the other end of the camp, came the faint, jingling sounds of music and laughter.

'Stay with you,' she said, and lay down against his side. There passed a long stretch of time without either of them speaking. She listened to her father's heavy, sore breathing, to the snoring of her brother, and the whispering of the burning wood flaking in the fire. The fire was dying, and the shadows grew darker and larger. From outside, from far away, and quietened by the damp evening, came the sound of others laughing and laughing.

'You can't tell me a story,' the girl whispered, 'so I'll tell you one.' She put one hand under her cheek and the other across his hot body, where it rode up and down, up and down on his sharp rib-cage. 'I'll tell you a story to make you better, a *mending* story. I'll tell you – *The Boy and the Blacksmith*.'

Once, Linnet-me-Dad, there was this blacksmith, and a damn good blacksmith he was. He could make anything in iron, and he knowed his own worth.

He was tending to his business, this blacksmith, working away in his forge, when up there comes a man all dressed in velvets and silks,

3

with leather shoes on his feet and leather gloves on his hands, and a feathered hat on his head. He was leading a horse that had dropped a shoe.

'Ar, I'll soon fix that for you,' says Blacksmith. 'Nobody can shoe hoss as well and quick as me. You stand you there and wait, and you won't believe how quick I'll be.'

So Blacksmith hammered away – tang! dong! – and the iron glowed and the sparks flew; and he set the hot shoe to the hoof and the smoke went up. To the gentleman he says, 'And what do *you* do to put bread on your table?' He was a blacksmith, and a good un, and he'd speak as he pleased to anybody.

'Funny thing, but I'm a smith too,' says the gentleman. 'A goldsmith.'

'Oh, you'll be making rings and brooches and such trash, then,' says Blacksmith. 'Are you any good?'

'The King seems satisfied,' said the gentleman. 'I'm the King's goldsmith.'

'I bet you do well for yourself, then?' says Blacksmith. 'I wouldn't be happy, meself, tapping with little hammers and making such finicky tawdries. A ploughshare! That's a piece of work, and it turns the earth for the seed! A sickle, a scythe! Them's work; and they cut the harvest. My work feeds the country! You – why you can't even shoe your own hoss! Aye,' he said, as he finished shoeing the hoss, 'if the King had any sense he'd dress his blacksmiths in velvets.'

Well, the goldsmith listened to all this, and he said nothing; and when his hoss was shoed, off he rode.

Off he went to the King's palace, and first

chance he got, he says to the King, 'I met a blacksmith on my travels, your majesty, who shoed my horse, and told me my work was finicky trash, and that he was a better man than me.' And he told the King all about the blacksmith.

The King laughed and said, 'I'd like to meet this blacksmith who fancies dressing in velvets. Send for him – we'll have a competition between him and you. If he wins, perhaps I'll make him Royal Blacksmith, and give him a suit of velvet working clothes – black velvet, so it won't show the dirt.'

Straightaway a messenger was sent to the blacksmith, to tell him to come to the King. Blacksmith says to himself, 'That goldsmith wasn't such a bad un after all – he's put in a good word for me with the King, and the King wants to reward me.' He shut up his forge, put on his best clothes and his strongest boots, and set off to walk to London.

So there was the blacksmith on the tramp, tramp, tramp – a big, strong man, planting his feet down hard on the road and swinging along. And up comes another tramp and falls in with him – a boy, a skinny, scruffy, navvy-boy, down on his luck and out of work. No boots to his feet and hardly a coat to his back. Hair hanging round his face all rough knife-chopped. He looks at Blacksmith; Blacksmith looks at him. 'Where are you going?' says the navvy-boy.

'What's it to you?' says Blacksmith.

'Ah, go on, tell me, man, tell me.'

'Well, I'm going to the King,' says Blacksmith. 'I'm going to be the King's own blacksmith and

5

make his ploughshares and wear velvets and silk. So sling your hook! I don't want any raggedy-arsed, scrounging, shiftless, whining beggars hanging round me.'

But the navvy-boy didn't clear off. He tagged along behind Blacksmith. 'You might need some help when you get to the King,' he said.

'Come the day I need your help, Heaven'll fall,' said Blacksmith.

On they tramped and on, until they come to London and the King's palace. The blacksmith was showed in to the King, and the goldsmith was there as well, standing by the throne and smirking.

'I hear you're the best blacksmith living,' says the King.

The blacksmith bowed his head and said, 'One of 'em, I'm one of 'em, for sure.'

'I hear you think you're worth more than my goldsmith here.'

'That's only sense,' says Blacksmith. 'What I make is useful. What he makes is just glitter and clutter.'

'Well,' says the King, 'we're going to have a contest to decide. You'll each make three things, and the one who's judged to have made the better things – I'll make him a rich man.'

'I'm a rich man then,' says Blacksmith. 'Nobody but a fool'd judge a goldsmith's work above a blacksmith's. Gold can't keep an edge.'

'Ah,' said the goldsmith, 'but gold can't rust either.'

Contest started the next day. Blacksmith was given a forge with every tool he'd need, and many rods of iron to work with; and the

6

goldsmith went into his workshop. Blacksmith got his fire started and thought he would make a horseshoe – four horseshoes. 'Without shoes, hosses can't work,' he said. 'Carts wouldn't get pulled, fields wouldn't get ploughed, and how would we get on then? Hoss-shoes have got to beat anything the goldsmith can make.'

He was hammering away at his horseshoes when into his forge come the scruffy, skinny, raggedy-arsed navvy-boy. 'You again!' says Blacksmith. 'Sling your hook!'

'Have you seen what Goldsmith's making?' the boy asks. 'Go and have a look. I'll keep the fire hot here.'

That made Blacksmith curious, so he left the boy working the bellows, and went over to the goldsmith's workshop to see what he was at. On the goldsmith's table stood a tiny apple tree. It had golden roots growing from a lump of beautiful green stone, and its trunk was gold, twisted just like a living tree. It was in full leaf, and every leaf was fine green gold, and they moved at a breath. Polished, shining apples of red gold hung among the leaves. And more wonderful than all this – the tree was alive. It was quick to grow, being so small, and Blacksmith saw, with his own eyes, a blossom of white-gold fall, and a red-gold apple swell in its place.

'Pretty,' said Blacksmith. 'But what use?' And back he went to his own forge to finish his hoss-shoes.

When he ducked in, he found the navvy-boy at the anvil, beating at something with a hammer. 'What're you at?' says Blacksmith, and

7

drags the boy out of it by what was left of his jacket.

On the anvil was a deer, lifting its head and spreading its spindly legs to struggle to its feet like a newborn fawn. Black and silver it was, a coat of soot-black iron, and a breast and rump of hammer-polished silver.

'Not bad,' says Blacksmith, 'but its head aint quite right – come here.' And he reached for the tongs the boy held the deer in, and for the hammer. The boy give them up to him, and Blacksmith plunged the deer into the fire and, when it was glowing a dull red, started working it again. 'More of a slope to its shoulders – like that. Tail smaller – so. Now!' he says, splashing the deer into the water-tub and bringing it back to the anvil. 'That's a deer.'

And the beautiful little iron deer walked with titupping steps to the edge of the anvil and looked down at the floor. 'Take it away,' says Blacksmith. 'I've got to finish me hoss-shoes.'

'Take the deer to the contest,' says the boy. 'The hoss-shoes are fine hoss-shoes – but who'll look at hoss-shoes when they see the golden apple tree?'

'That's as maybe,' says Blacksmith, and got to work on his hoss-shoes and finished them. But when it was time to go to the King for the judging, Blacksmith wrapped the deer as well as the hoss-shoes, in an old piece of sacking, and carried them along with him.

Goldsmith brought along a parcel wrapped in purple silk, and set it on a table before the King. When he took away the silk, there was a box of polished golden oak; and when he took off the lid and let down the sides of the box, there stood the little tree; and everybody there said, 'O-o-h,' all together, like a breeze, it was so beautiful. As they all stared, down from the tree fell an over-ripe apple of red gold. It broke on the green stone, and a smell of apples and gold filled the room. Through the window came a wasp, a real wasp, and it hovered and flew around the broken apple.

The King couldn't take his eyes off the tree, but he said, 'Blacksmith; can you show us anything more rare than this?'

Blacksmith threw his sacking down on the floor with a clash and clang of iron that made the whole court jump and look round. Out from underneath the sacking, its little iron hooves sounding like little hammers on the stone floor, ran the black and silver deer. Blacksmith caught it and said, 'There's this toy here –' And he dumped it on the table beside the apple tree, out of his way. 'And then there's my hoss-shoes – see? Four good hoss-shoes that'll shoe a cart-hoss, a plough-hoss or a war-hoss – and I can make you hundreds more, just as good.'

But nobody was listening because everybody was watching the lovely little deer, so lovely in every way it moved. It reached up its head and nibbled the green-gold leaves of the apple tree – and when it had eaten all the leaves it could reach, it started on the tree's golden bark. It nibbled and nibbled all round the trunk – and the apple tree withered. Gold don't tarnish, and it stayed as bright as ever – but the leaves fell or shrivelled, and the red-gold fruit fell, until the golden branches were bare. Iron is stronger than gold.

9

The King and the judges talked together, and they decided that they had to give the prize to Blacksmith, because he had made the deer *and* the hoss-shoes.

The raggedy-arsed navvy-boy was waiting outside for Blacksmith. 'Did you win?' he said.

"Course I did,' says Blacksmith.

On the second day of the contest Blacksmith went to his forge thinking that he would make a scythe blade. 'With a good sharp edge. A scythe blade – mow the grass to make hay, feed the beasts through the winter. Cut the corn to make bread. What would we eat without good sharp scythe blades?'

So he got his fire going and he started making a scythe blade. But in comes the ragged boy and says, 'You should see what Goldsmith's making.'

'Look what I'm making,' says Blacksmith.

'It's as good a scythe as anybody could make – but you see what Goldsmith's making.'

'Keep the fire hot,' says Blacksmith, and off he went to the goldsmith's forge.

On the goldsmith's table lay a fish, made all of gold and silver. A great round silver eye, it had, and silver fins; and its scales rippled through all the shades of gold: green and russet, buttercup and corn. It was even studded here and there with an emerald or a ruby. Up came its tail and went slap! on the table. Its mouth and gills opened and shut.

Blacksmith turned and walked away, saying, 'But a scythe – a scythe's useful.'

In his own forge the boy was at work. 'Come out of there, and let me finish me scythe.'

'You'll have plenty of time for that. Help me finish this.'

'What is it?'

'An otter,' says the boy.

'Come here,' says Blacksmith, taking the hammer from the boy. 'That's never an otter. Look, you want the tail more like this –' Bang! went the hammer. K-dang! Kang! 'And the feet more – !' Into the fire went the otter and out, glowing, on to the anvil. 'And the back, you've got the back wrong, you've never seen an otter!'

And, as the boy watched, Blacksmith shaped the iron into a humping back, a slinking tail – and the tail began to wave, the nose to lift and twitch, and it was a true otter that crouched on the anvil, still hot from the fire. An iron otter, streaked rust red, with soot-black feet and a soot-black tip to its tail.

'Fine work,' says the boy; and Blacksmith grinned. He doused the otter, sizzling, in his water-tub, and got on with his scythe blade. When he had done, he wrapped otter and scythe blade in his piece of old sacking and set off to the place of judging. It was outside that day, by one of the palace pools.

Before the King and court, Goldsmith unfolded a length of white silk, and showed them his gold and silver fish. It flapped, sparkled and glared in the sunlight, and leapt from Goldsmith's arms into the pool. The King leaned forward from his chair to watch its scales flashing through the green water of the pool, and gleaming as it leapt.

'Blacksmith, have you anything to show more rare than this?' asks the King.

11

Blacksmith threw down his sacking-wrapped bundle with a crash that made people cover their ears. The otter had been wriggling to escape, and now it threw off the sacking, ran to the edge of the pond and dived in. 'There's that otter,' said Blacksmith, 'but here's my real piece of work – a scythe blade. It'll take an edge and it'll hold an edge; it'll balance, it'll swing. Get in your hay-harvest and your corn-harvest with that.'

The King and court weren't listening. They were stooping over the pool, watching the iron otter swoop and swerve through the water after the gold and silver fish. The fish dodged, the fish dashed, but the otter was behind, above, upon – and the otter climbed out of the pool at the King's feet, with the fish in its mouth. The water ran from the otter in red, rusty streams, and they could see that the beast was made of iron, living iron. Iron is stronger than gold.

And again the winner was declared to be Blacksmith, because the golden fish was soon hidden inside the otter, and the otter and the scythe had been made by Blacksmith.

'What will you make tomorrow?' asked the raggedy navvy-boy, who was waiting for Blacksmith at the front of the watching crowd.

'A ploughshare,' says Blacksmith. 'It's what I make best, and what can be better than a ploughshare? You can't plough, you can't plant seed, you can't eat bread without a ploughshare.'

And, next day, Blacksmith started to make a ploughshare. But when the navvy-boy come into his forge and said, 'You should see what Goldsmith's making,' he left his work straight off, and went over to Goldsmith's shop.

A crown was what Goldsmith was making, a crown made like a wreath of corn, all of gold: gold stems and gold leaves, and golden heads of grain, that all bent when you touched them like the living grass. Blacksmith turned on his heel and went back to his forge to see what the boy was making. It was something a bit bird shaped. Blacksmith put his hands on his hips. 'What the Hell is that?'

'A cockerel?' says the boy.

'Get out me way. Haven't you never seen a bloody cockerel?' And Blacksmith heated the bird in the fire until it went from being a black cock to a red cock and then to a white cock. He pulled it out, banged it on the anvil and set to the hammering. He hammered out its long tail-feathers, he hammered out its wings; he heated it in the fire again and hammered out its beak and comb and feet. He doused it in the water-tub, sending up a sizzle and a cloud of steam, and then he put it on the anvil, where it fluffed up its red and black feathers.

The boy put out his hand and ruffled the wet, hot feathers. They were iron, and crinkled and rustled as he stroked them, but they were almost as soft as a real cock's feathers. 'Fine work,' he says, but Blacksmith swept the iron cock from the anvil, and made his ploughshare.

At the judging, Goldsmith brought in his work on a black velvet cushion covered by a square of black silk. He set the cushion on a table before the King and court, whisked off the silk, and there lay the golden wreath of golden corn, shining, beautiful. But the King and court only drew in their breaths once before their eyes turned to Blacksmith, and the bundle of sacking he held in his arms.

'Blacksmith?' says the King, and winced as Blacksmith crashed down his bundle on the marble floor. The sacking moved, it flounced, and from under it came the iron cock, batting its wings and strutting, arching its neck, stretching its beak, raising its comb.

'There's that bird,' says Blacksmith, crouching to unwrap the rest of the sacking, 'but here, look at this. A ploughshare! Now that's your work. That's as good a ploughshare as you'll find anywhere. That'll see a man out, that ploughshare. That'll feed a county.'

But while Blacksmith praised his ploughshare, the King and court were watching the cock. It danced up to the golden corn wreath, and pecked and pecked and gobbled down the seeds, trampled on it and tore off the grain, chased each rolling seed and ate it. And when the golden wreath was torn and stripped of all its heads, then the cock flapped its wings, stretched up its neck and gave an iron crow. Iron is stronger than gold.

The King and court had to declare Blacksmith the winner that day too, because he had not only made the iron cock, but the ploughshare too. So Blacksmith won all three contests, and was the winner; and the King made him the Royal Blacksmith, and gave him a house in the palace, and a workshop of his own. The blacksmith didn't dress in silks and velvets, but he had more money in his pocket, wore better clothes and ate better food than he ever had before.

'Come and live with me,' he said to the

raggedy-arsed navvy-boy. 'There's plenty of room in my house, plenty of food on the table.'

'I'm a navvy,' said the boy. 'I'm used to the tramp. But I'll come and eat with you if I'm ever on the tramp this way again.'

So the boy tramped off, and Blacksmith stayed to make shoes for all the King's horses, buckles for all the King's men, hoes and rakes for the King's gardeners, bolts for the King's doors, and lengths of chain, buckets, nails, strongboxes, cooking pots, and anything else of iron that was needed. Now and again he thought of making something that wasn't useful at all, but only good to look at, like the things he had made with the boy, but then he would think, 'Why bother?'

So time went on, and Goldsmith, who hadn't forgotten how he'd been beaten, started saying, 'Isn't it strange that Blacksmith never makes anything as wonderful as he made when first he came here? No more iron deer, otters, cockerels. Perhaps he can't make them. Perhaps he didn't make those first ones.'

And people began to wonder if Blacksmith deserved his house and his wage from the King. It was just at this time that the navvy-boy come back to visit Blacksmith. He knocked on Blacksmith's door and said, 'Can I use the forge?'

'Aye,' said Blacksmith, and went out with him to see why the boy needed the forge. Tethered to the forge's doorpost were the two worst hosses Blacksmith had ever seen. They were old and bony. Their long necks hung down. They were knock-kneed. Their coats were as rough as ragrugs. The raggedy boy got the fire going, then took sledge-hammer and saw, chisel and wedge.

'Stand back,' he said. 'There'll be some blood.'
And then he broke both hosses into pieces. The
blood did fly.

When it had stopped flying, the boy sorted
among the pieces and chose the best. He put
them into the fire and heated them white hot. He
banged them on the anvil and beat them with the
hammer. He beat head on to neck, neck on to
withers. He beat the legs straight, he beat the
coat smooth, he did a job of work.

Blacksmith had wanted to run away when the
hosses were broken up, but the forging he knew,
and he watched close. The boy wasn't as good a
smith as him, but he was good, he was good.
And the boy forged, from those two sorry hosses, one fine and handsome hoss. 'Thank you for
your forge,' he says, as he led that fine hoss
away.

Blacksmith went back into his house and
thought much about what he'd seen. The boy
had done nothing that he couldn't do. And when
people went on saying that Blacksmith had
cheated, Blacksmith went to the King and said, 'I
hear the gossip about me. Give me the two best
hosses from your stable, and you'll see what I
can do. I shall take them two hosses and forge
them into one hoss: the best hoss in the world.'

The best hoss in the world. The King wanted
that – and this blacksmith was a man who could
take a lump of iron and make a living cockerel
and a ploughshare in one day. So the King said,
'Have my two best horses given to the blacksmith.' And he went along to Blacksmith's forge
to see the forging of one hoss out of two.

When Blacksmith saw the King and all the

court gather around his forge, and he saw the two beautiful hosses, and thought of what he had to try and do, his guts rolled. But then he thought: I'm a better smith than that raggedy-arsed navvy-boy, and if he can make one hoss out of two, then I can. So, without thinking about it any more, Blacksmith took an axe, and a hammer and a saw, and he attacked the two hosses, and cut them into pieces.

The court sat there, watching, all bespattered with blood and hair. Blacksmith wiped his bloody face, smiled at the King, and hauled the hoss pieces into the forge. He plunged the pieces into the fire – but instead of glowing and softening, they burned. He held them on the anvil and battered them, and all he made was a mess.

The King watched, and smelt the roasting hoss-flesh, and he was the angrier minute by minute, not only because his two hosses were dead, but because Blacksmith had made a fool of him. 'Arrest that man,' he said. 'Throw him in the deepest dungeon.'

'But I did everything that *he* did, and I'm the better smith,' said Blacksmith, as the soldiers came and lifted him up from among the pieces of hoss.

Into the deepest dungeon Blacksmith was thrown. It was grey and dark in there, the only light coming from one tiny window too high in the wall to reach. Cold water ran down the cold, stone walls, and Blacksmith's clothes were soon cold and soaked, and he was chilled through. To make him more miserable, the only company he had, down there in the cold dark, was a dying man, who lay on the wet floor coughing, sweating and shivering, and didn't even know the blacksmith was there.

That very same night, the raggedy-arsed navvy-boy come into the dungeon. Straight through the stone wall he come, carrying a heap of firewood in his arms. He piled the wood up in the middle of the dungeon, spat a flame out of his mouth, and lit a good hot fire.

'Thank you!' says Blacksmith, and he huddled close to the fire, but the boy had already jumped back through the wall.

Blacksmith dragged the dying man close to the fire too, so that he could at least die warm. The boy come twice more, bringing more firewood the first time, and then a big iron cauldron and a tripod. 'Set that up over the fire,' the boy said, and jumped through the wall again.

Blacksmith set the tripod over the fire, and waited to see what would happen next. Back come the boy with two buckets of water. He emptied one into the cauldron. 'Hang that over the fire,' he said, and Blacksmith did. The boy emptied the other bucket of water into it. 'Keep the fire hot,' he said. 'The water must boil.' And away he went through the wall.

Blacksmith watched the fire, ready to put on more wood. But the boy soon come back, carrying a big cleaver and a long stick. He sat down by the fire with Blacksmith and the dying man, and waited until the water boiled in the cauldron. Blacksmith didn't like to ask what was going on, but he watched everything.

When the water was roiling, bubbling and boiling in the cauldron, the boy got up, the cleaver in his hand, and went over to the dying man. He took the man's hair in his hand and, with one chop, cut off his head. Blacksmith started, but knew enough by now to keep quiet and watch.

There was no blood. The boy took the head and threw it into the boiling water. He took up the long stick and he began to stir the head round and round. Blacksmith listened closely, but the boy said nothing as he stirred and stirred like a housewife stirring a stew.

After some minutes of stirring, the boy asked Blacksmith to help him lift the cauldron off the fire because it was too heavy for him alone.

'Not for me,' said Blacksmith and, stripping off his shirt to wrap around the cauldron's handle, he lifted the big pot off the fire and set it on the dungeon's stone floor.

'Now we wait for it to cool,' said the boy and, when it had, he lifted the head out by the hair, and stuck it back on the neck of the man he had chopped it off. The man sat up and looked around. He wasn't coughing, he wasn't shivering. He was well, Dad, he was cured.

The boy overturned the cauldron over the fire and put it out. Then he carried everything away through the wall, until there was no sign that he'd been there except a cured man and a little more water, and hotter water, on the floor than there had been – and nobody'd notice that except them who had to sit in it.

As for Blacksmith, he didn't have a chance to say hello to the other prisoner before the door of the dungeon opened and guards came in to take the cured man away. 'You've been pardoned,' they said to him.

'What about me?' Blacksmith asked.

'You?' said the guards. 'The King's trying to think up a way of executing you that's as bad as you deserve. You stay here.'

There, in the cold, dark, wet dungeon, Blacksmith stayed. He counted the days passing by watching the little window high in his wall, and the number of times his guards brought him bread and water. One day seemed endless, and two more than he could bear, but he bore three, and then four, five, six, and then he'd been a whole week in prison. He wasn't used to being so cold and wet, or doing so little work, or eating only bread and water. 'Soon I won't have the strength to make a nail,' he thought. 'I wish the King would execute me if he's going to execute me.' And he said to his guards, 'Hasn't the King decided how to have me killed yet?'

'Oh the King was so mad over what you did,' said the guard, 'that he's fallen into a brain fever. He's raving. Think yourself lucky. Until he's well, you live.'

Day by day the guard brought Blacksmith news of the King's sickness, of how doctor after doctor had tried to save him and had failed, and now the doctors were scared to try. The King was dying.

Blacksmith had plenty of time to sit in his dungeon and think of all this. 'The King's angry with me now,' he thought, 'but if I saved his life, he'd have to forgive me. And if I did just what the boy did with the cauldron . . . I made a mess of the hosses,' he thought, 'but maybe I missed something. Now I *know* that I saw everything the boy did with the cauldron, and it was easy. Just off with his head, into the boiling water, stir, stir, and then back on his neck again. Can't go wrong. And what other choice do I have? Either sit here and wait for this King or the next to execute me, or do something to save myself.'

So he decided and, the next time the guard came, Blacksmith said, 'I can save your King. No one else can do it, but I can. Let me try – what have you to lose? Tell them up there – I can save the King.'

The guard went away, and told his superior officers what Blacksmith said, and they told their superior officers, who came to hear what Blacksmith had to say for themselves. And then they went away and told the courtiers and advisers, who came themselves to listen to Blacksmith, and in the end it was decided to let Blacksmith try and save the King, because nobody else could do it, so what had they to lose?

Blacksmith was brought out of his dungeon and taken to the King's room, all filthy and wet, just as he was. The King lay in his bed, tossing and moaning and shivering.

'You must do just as I say and bring me everything I ask for,' said Blacksmith. 'Build that fire up – fetch me a cauldron and a tripod – and water – and the biggest kitchen cleaver you've got – and the big spoon that the cook stirs the porridge with.'

Away went the servants at a run, and they brought back firewood and soon had a big fire burning up the chimney. They brought back a tripod and set it up over the fire. They brought a kitchen cauldron, filled it with water and hung it on the tripod. And they brought a big kitchen cleaver, and the long wooden spoon that the cook used to stir enough porridge for the whole palace.

'Good,' said Blacksmith. 'Now, everybody out!' And he herded them all from the room and shut the door on them.

'Now then,' he said to himself. 'First get the water boiling.' He watched the water until it boiled. Then he picked up the kitchen cleaver and went over to the bed. He gripped the King by the hair, but he didn't feel happy. 'It's what the boy did,' he told himself, and whack! he chopped off the King's head.

But there was a lot of blood, all over the royal bed. 'There was no blood when the boy did it,' said Blacksmith. 'Still . . . better get on.' So he took the head and threw it into the boiling water. He took up the porridge spoon and began stirring. But it wasn't right, it wasn't right. The prisoner's head hadn't cooked.

Blacksmith used the spoon to help him get the head out of the cauldron. He scalded his hands, but didn't care. Quickly he carried the King's head to the bed and tried to fit it back on to the neck. But the head wouldn't take. Again and again it rolled soggily on the bedclothes, away from the neck.

Blacksmith sat on the floor beside the bed, sat in streams of blood, and put his head in his hands. 'I did everything the boy did. *Everything*,' he said. 'I wish that boy was here, I wish he was, raggedy-arsed little cuss that he is.'

Something brushed against him, and he looked up, and it was the boy's trouser leg. The boy was leaning over Blacksmith to reach the

King's head. He crossed the room and tossed it back into the boiling water. 'Mop up all the blood with the bedsheets,' he said, 'and put them in the pot too.'

Blacksmith jumped to help. The bedsheets were already soaked in blood, and he dragged them off the bed, letting the King's body fall on the floor, and he mopped up as much blood as he could from the floor with the sheets and with the pillowcases. Then he stuffed the sheets and the pillowcases into the boiling water with the King's head, while the boy stirred and stirred with the long wooden spoon.

'Now take the pot off the fire,' – and the two them heaved the pot off the tripod. The boy hooked the sheets and pillowcases out of the pot with the spoon and threw them on the floor, where they soaked the rugs and steamed. When the water was a little cooler, he lifted out the King's head by the hair, carried it over to the King's body, and fitted it to the King's neck. It stuck there at once, and the King sat up and looked around.

'Blacksmith!' he said, and scowled.

The boy opened the door, and let in all the courtiers who had been waiting outside. 'The blacksmith has saved you!' they called out. And they crowded around the King – who was sitting in his nightshirt amongst the soggy sheets on the floor, with hot water dripping out of his hair – and told him how ill he had been, how the doctors had given up trying to cure him, but that Blacksmith had saved him. And while they were all talking, the raggedy-arsed boy went away, and no one saw him go.

Well, the King couldn't execute Blacksmith after that; it would have been ungrateful. But he still remembered his horses, and he didn't want Blacksmith around his palace any more. So he give him a satchel full of gold as a reward, and sent him home to his village and his old forge. 'And think yourself lucky!' said the King.

So there was Blacksmith on the tramp, tramp again, walking out of the city with his satchel of gold on his shoulder. And along comes the raggedy-arsed navvy-boy and falls in with him.

'Here you are again,' said Blacksmith. 'I owe you something. You want this gold? You earned it.'

'It's too heavy to carry on the tramp,' said the boy. 'But if you want to give me something . . .'

'Just say what you want.'

'Some shoes would be good,' said the boy. 'My feet get cold and sore.'

'You shall have the best pair of shoes money can buy,' said Blacksmith.

'And me hands get cold too.'

'And some gloves, best that can be got.'

So they stopped at a leather shop, and Blacksmith ordered shoes for the boy, and gloves. The boy hopped up on to the counter, and when the shoes were brought, Blacksmith took them from the shopkeeper and himself put them on the boy's feet. And it was strange, but there was a hole, that might have been made by one of Blacksmith's own nails, through both of the boy's feet. But Blacksmith laced up the shoes and then the holes couldn't be seen.

Then the shopkeeper brought the gloves and Blacksmith tugged them on to the boy's hands.

There was a hole through each of the boy's wrists, but the gloves buttoned over them.

The boy kissed Blacksmith, jumped down from the counter and clattered out of the shop in his new shoes. Blacksmith paid the shopkeeper, and then went on his way to his village, home to his village, home, where he walked by his cold forge, and opened up his cold house, and went in, and lay down, and slept . . . and woke up to make hoss-shoes, and ploughshares, and scythes, and nails and buckets and bolts and pots for the rest of his life.

'There's no more,' said the girl. 'That's all there is to that story.'

Linnet, shivering again, could say nothing, but he had listened to it all. When he had been as cold, even at the centre of his bones, as if lying at the bottom of a frozen winter ditch, he had listened gratefully; and when he had been shivering, and as hot and wet as if he had been boiling in the boy's cauldron, he had still listened. Through the hot ache of his head had come his daughter's voice, and her words had made, in the red darkness of the hut, leaping golden fish and iron deer, and living heads swirling in stirred pots, which were better things to think of than sore throats and sore lungs.

'Dost want a drink?' she asked.

'I want – when I'm dead – you to cut off me head and carry it home.'

The girl laughed and, soon after, fell asleep beside him on the damp bed. In the dark corner, the little boy still snored. And from far away, struggling through the thick thump of blood in his head, came the sound of music from the wedding.

The distant noise quietened slowly, as the fire died, and the darkness in the bothy grew blacker and stank of ashes; and the cold became sharper. Then there was the sound of tramping feet nearby, the flap of the door-curtain, and a breeze which made the last embers of the fire glow red in the blackness. A shuffle, a thump and an angry, mumbling voice: a sound of breathing and scuffling, and a heavy weight crashed on to the legs of the sick man and the girl.

'Mind!' rasped the sick man, his voice like the tearing of cloth.

'Wha'? Who's that?' A hand, smelling of sweat and gin, came groping over the sick man's chest and face, like a fleshy spider. 'Bloody Hellfire, Linnet, mate, you'm hot as a coal!'

'Bullhead?' Linnet said. 'Bullhead, listen – '

'What you need's a swig o' this, mate,' Bullhead said, and there was a liquid sound, a bubbling of liquor in a bottle. 'Here – '

Linnet painfully raised up his head, took hold of the bottle that Bullhead still held and drank down gin. 'Oh God,' he said, lying back.

'Told you – feel better. Me coat –?' Bullhead felt for his own coat – or, at any rate, a coat – from among those covering Linnet and the girl. He needed it to keep himself warm in bed.

'Bullhead, listen . . . I'm dying.'

'No! – Not that, mate! Worse than you – '

'I'm dying,' Linnet said. 'Do summat for me when I'm dead.'

Bullhead sprawled himself over Linnet's legs and drank from his bottle. 'What would that be, mate?'

'Cut me head off.'

'Cut your –? Cut your –?' In the darkness, a deep rough sound – Bullhead laughing.

'Listen . . . listen,' Linnet whispered. 'Want me babbies to go home.'

'Don't worrit about the babbies, mate!' Bullhead spilled some of his gin on Linnet's coverings as he gestured expansively and unseen in the dark. 'Somebody'll take 'em in.'

'No.' Linnet was weary and sore. 'No. Don't want 'em here. Go home. My mother – will look after 'em.'

'Good! Good!' Bullhead said, thumping Linnet's legs.

'Cut off my head. Carry it with 'em.'

'All right, mate, all right,' Bullhead said, slapping him on the chest. 'I'll cut off your head, right enough.' To another man, unknown in the darkness, who fell in through the doorway, Bullhead called out, 'I'm to chop Linnet's head off when he's dead.'

The next day, the navvies leaving the hut were stopped by Linnet's hand fumbling at their ankles, and his plea that they should cut his head off when he died. When they returned that night, he was past saying anything sensible, but when he died, there were too many men and women, besides his daughter, to swear to what his last request had been for it to be ignored. His head was cut off by the camp's butcher, before the body was taken on a cart to an anonymous grave in the nearest churchyard. 'Pig's head, man's head, what's the differ?' said the butcher, and whacked down his cleaver.

About what to do with the head once it was off, there was less agreement.

'Linnet wanted us to go home and take him with us,' said the girl, Linnet's daughter. Few knew her name. She was, like her brother, 'Linnet's Babby' to most, though Linnet's gang called her 'First Born', because Linnet had.

'But Lamb,' said a woman, 'how am you to do it? Do you know where your granny lives? How am you to get there?'

The girl held her brother's hand, and was obstinately silent.

'Stay here with we,' said the woman. 'You can muck in with us all. As for your Daddy's head, we'll put it up there – ' She looked upwards into the few rafters of the hut. 'It'll smoke like a pig's head, I reckon.'

The little girl said nothing, but didn't change her mind. She took the best of her father's clothes, and all of his tools, and sold them to the camp's shop, and so got a little money in her pocket. And, when no one was watching, she claimed a loaf of bread, giving it to her brother to carry. She wrapped their father's head in his old working shirt, and tied the sleeves into a handle and then, taking her brother by the hand, she led him out of the hut and out of the camp.

They walked away from the village of huts, with its rubbish heaps and smoking fires. They walked away from the great ugly gash cut through the earth for the canal. They passed the heaps of loose earth thrown out of the ditch, brown and black heaps, patched and streaked

28

with creamy clay, and smelling richly of mud.

For yards away from the ditch the earth was naked, scoured of every leaf of grass, every bush, every flower; and for yards more the greenery was bespattered by earth, daubed with mud, buried under spoil-banks. But, beyond that, they began to climb a grassy hill slope, and ahead of them hawthorn flowers shone white against green leaves and black twigs.

As they passed the hawthorns, and climbed higher over the tree-bare top of the hill, First Born told Little Un the story he'd slept through, to draw his attention from the home they were leaving behind them. 'And there was Blacksmith, on the tramp, tramp, tramp – '

The hill sloped gently, slowly up, and as gently down the other side. A deep lane ran around the bottom of the hill, fringed by another row of squat hawthorn bushes. There, beneath the black-branched trees, with their bright green leaves and foaming clusters of starry white flowers, First Born sat down with Little Un, and untied the shirt.

The cloth fell away from the head, which lay there, its eyes closed, its lips barely parted, cushioned on its own thick, long, dark hair. The face so well known, but now so strange.

'Dadda,' said the girl. 'Linnet.'

The head's eyes opened, the dark lashes lifting slowly from the faint blue shadow under the brown skin, the lids rolling slowly upwards to reveal the amber and russet of the brown eyes beneath. The lips drew back from the teeth in a smile.

'Which way do we go, Dadda?'

Linnet's eyes moved as he looked at the haw-thorns. 'The lane below here – follow that – and go over Broomfield Hill beyond there – then you'll be on your way.'

'When we've had a rest,' said First Born, and the children lay on either side of the head, and ate bread, and listened while the head finished the story.

'And whack! he cut off the man's head, and dropped it in the cauldron and boiled it up . . .'

2

The men were navvies – that much could be told by the dirt caked on their trousers, and by the spike of a pick which stuck out from the sacking-wrapped bundle one carried on his shoulder. They had tired of life on one diggings and, hearing that diggers were wanted in another place, they had set out on the tramp.

They were picking their way down Broomfield Hill, their feet and ankles hidden in the grass, and the grass-heads thrashing against their mud-hardened trousers, when the first man stopped suddenly, and his friend walked into him. The first man nodded at what he had seen.

They had rounded a clump of dark green, spiny broom, covered with bright yellow flowers and there, in its shelter, sat a small, dirty girl, and a dirty, even smaller boy. Each was eating a lump of bread torn from the loaf that lay in the grass in front of them.

'Hello sweetheart!' said the smaller of the two men to the girl. 'What have you got there?'

The girl held up her bread and smiled. She was a little shy of them, but not afraid.

'Having a bit to eat, eh? Got some to spare for me mate and me? We aint et since this morning.'

The girl leaned forward, picked up the loaf and held it out to them. The two men looked at each other, grinned, threw down their loads of tools and clothes, and shambled over to drop down in the grass beside the boy and girl. The bigger man tore the loaf in two and shared it between himself and his friend, and grinned when he saw the girl look shocked at that.

'We got bigger appetites than little bits like you,' he said.

'And what are you doing here, all by your lonesomes?' the smaller man asked, chewing on his bread. 'I suppose your mam and your dad are somewhere about?'

The girl nodded, but the little boy said, 'Dad's dead.'

'Ah,' said the man, tipping back his head, and grinning down his nose at the girl. 'Dad's dead, is he?'

'Hey, there's a good shirt here,' said the other man, and reached for it.

The girl grabbed it. 'My dad's shirt.'

'Well, he won't be wanting it any more, will he?' The man tugged at the shirt, and there was a clink and rattle. The man, still holding the shirt, turned to look at his friend. 'Money,' he said.

'Money, sweetheart!' said the other man. 'How much you got?'

'None!' said the girl.

'Oh, now, you mustn't tell lies, sweetheart, it's naughty. And, because you're so naughty –' The man got up and stepped over to his friend and the bundle, where he crouched down to feel it. There was another clink of money. 'Good shirt – an' there's summat else wrapped up in here – a pair of boots, sweetheart?' As he spoke, he untied the bundle and unfolded the shirt – and sprang up and back with a cry. The bigger man, too, threw himself backwards on the grass.

At the centre of the unfolded shirt lay the head, its thick dark hair curling about its face, its mouth smiling in its greying beard, and its open brown eyes seeming to look at them. The man who had uncovered it fell to his knees and covered his mouth with his hands.

As the men gaped, the little girl, kneeling, lifted the head between her hands and set it on her lap. She combed its hair with her fingers, and the head's smile widened. The two men groaned aloud with fear, and groaned again when its eyes moved from one to the other of them.

'Take my babbies' bread, brothers,' said the head (and that silenced them). 'Take it all. Take the money. And while you eat it, and while you count it, I'll tell you a story to while away the time. I'll tell you – *Old Favours are Soon Forgotten*.'

There was this navvy, a poor hard-done-by navvy, down on his luck and out of work, trudging along the road, on the tramp from one diggings to the next. Brothers, he was so hungry, he'd sold his tools to buy food, and all he had to his name was the empty sack they'd been in. He kept it to wrap himself in at night.

Well, he's tramping along this lane when he hears horses' hoofs thumping the ground, horns blowing, hounds yelping – there's a hunt. And then, through the hedge at the side of the lane comes a wolf.

Now this wolf has been hard run. Its tongue was hanging out between its teeth, as dry as a stone. Its sides was going in and out, in and out, and all its ribs standing out an inch. Its paws were bleeding, and its fur was all dark and wet with sweat. This wolf looked at the navvy and it said, 'Help!'

The navvy, he knowed what it was like to be harried around by rich folk – don't we all, brothers? – so he took the sack off his back and held it open – and into the sack goes the wolf. The navvy heaves the sack on to his shoulder and on he goes.

Then up come the hounds, pouring through the hedge, crowding round the navvy's legs, all barking and baying. They kept jumping up at the sack, but the navvy kicks them off and wouldn't let them have it. And then up comes the horsemen, and the navvy shouts out, 'Oh, Masters, don't let your dogs have me dinner! I got a joint of pork that I worked for in me sack, that's all!'

'Which way did the wolf go?' says one of the horsemen, and the navvy pointed off over the hills – and the dogs were whipped off that way, and all the horsemen galloped after.

Navvy tramps on till he's sure he's well and away from the hunt. Then he stops, swings the sack down from his shoulder, and sets it on the ground. Out comes the wolf, feeling a lot stronger now, and licking his white teeth with his red tongue. 'Good of you to help me,' says the wolf. 'To show you I'm grateful, I'll kill you quick, if you'll keep still.'

'Kill me?' says Navvy.

'I need food after all that running,' says the wolf. 'You'll do.'

'But I saved your life!'

'You did,' says the wolf, 'but that's all past now, and old favours are soon forgotten.'

Well, Navvy stamps and he throws his sack down, and he says, 'Just like a wolf! Only a wolf could be so cruel. Men are kinder!'

'I've not seen much of men's kindness,' says the wolf.

'No man would kill and eat somebody who'd just saved his life. A man would give kindness for kindness.'

'I don't believe you,' says the wolf, 'and I'm still hungry . . . But I'll tell you what we'll do. We'll walk on along this road and the first one we meet, we'll ask 'em, are old favours remembered or forgotten? If they agree with you, I'll let you go. But if they agree with me . . .' And the wolf licked its chops again.

So it was a choice between visiting the Devil or the Devil's Granny, and Navvy went on along the lane with the wolf, and the first one they met was a creeping, limping old dog, with his tail and his ears drooped and a cough that shook him from nose to tail. And all his sides were cut, and flies was buzzing in packs about the blood.

'Good day to you, brother,' says the wolf. 'Let me ask you – are old favours remembered or forgotten?'

'Old favours are forgotten,' said the dog, and he lay down, tired out, in the dust. 'Brother, I've learned that if I've learned nothing else. For twenty years I guarded my master's yard, twenty long years. I kept away thieves and foxes – aye, and wolves an' all. I killed rats, I killed mice; I let his children pull me tail and ears and never bit – and I loved me master, and was happy to live on the scraps he didn't want, and what I could catch. But this morning, because I'm old and lame, because me teeth are broken and me bark worn out – this morning he chased me away with kicks and sharp stones – see how bad me sides are cut? Now I've no home and I'm too old to hunt. Now I must crawl along this roadside until I fall down and die, and me carcass'll lie in the ditch and be eaten by the rats, who hate me. Brother,' said the old dog, as he struggled to his feet again, 'take it from me: old favours are soon, soon forgotten.' And the old dog limped and crept away.

The wolf looked at Navvy and licked his chops.

'Listen, that was one man, and a rare cruel man!' said Navvy. 'Not one in a thousand would have treated the poor old dog like that! If he'd been mine, he'd have had a place by the fire, and pats and strokes, and all he could eat until he died in my bed! That on the man who turned him out, I say!' And Navvy spits on the road.

'Well,' says the wolf, 'I don't want it said that wolves aren't as fair as men, so let's go on a piece and ask the next one we meet. If they agree with you, I'll let you go. If they don't – dinner-time!'

Navvy was glad to go on living, even if only for another few minutes, and on they went. And the next one they met was an old horse, trudging along the road so slow and sad that her hooves made only a soft clop-clop in the dust. Her long bony neck drooped. Her mane and tail hung in knots, and her sides was all cut and bleeding with flies buzzing about the blood.

'Good day to you, sister,' says the wolf. 'Tell

us – are old favours remembered or forgotten?'

'Brother,' said the mare, 'old favours are forgotten. I know, I know! For twenty years I pulled my master's plough, for twenty years I pulled his cart – and all the reward I ever got was his whip on my back when the work was too hard. For twenty years I let his children kick me and climb on my back, and I never threw them off or kicked back. But this morning, because I'm old now and I've lost me strength – this morning he chased me off with kicks and sharp stones. And now I've nowhere to go, but shall just have to trudge along this road until I fall down and die, and the birds eat me. Brother, believe me when I tell you this: old favours are soon, soon forgotten.' And the old horse went plodding on.

The wolf looked at Navvy, and Navvy knew what it was thinking.

'A cruel man, a rare man – it must be the same man who turned out the dog! Not one man in ten thousand would have treated that poor horse so! If that horse had been mine, there would have been a warm stable and sunny field and a full manger for her until she died, I swear it!'

'I'll give you one more chance,' said the wolf, 'to show how fair wolves can be, even though I'm hungry enough now to eat two of you.'

So on they tramped, and came to a river and, as they walked by the river, they met a fox, a little vixen with a white tip to her tail, dancing along on thin black stockinged legs.

'Good day to you, sister,' says the wolf. 'Tell us, are old favours remembered or forgotten?'

Down sits Little Vixen in the road, and she looks at the wolf, and she looks at Navvy. 'A

37

funny question to ask, brothers,' says she. 'First you tell me – why do you ask it?'

'Easy enough told, sister,' says the wolf, and he told her all about how the navvy had rescued him from the hunt, and of the agreement they'd made, and of what the dog and the horse had said.

'A good story,' says Little Vixen, 'but I can't believe a big strong wolf like you could get into a small sack like that.'

The wolf was shamed at having hidden in the sack, and he only said, 'I was in it: enough.'

'But it's much too small. I think you're joking with me,' said Little Vixen. 'I won't believe you, or answer your question, unless I see you get in the sack.'

Navvy held open the sack, and Little Vixen waited, and flicked her tail – and at last the wolf got into the sack again, just to show that he could.

'Quick!' said Little Vixen. 'Tie the sack shut!' Navvy did as she said. 'Now quick! Chuck it in the river down there!'

Navvy heaved the sack in the air and down the bank. Through the air it flew, splashed into the river, and away downstream it was carried with the wolf drowning inside.

'There!' said Little Vixen, and danced in the road on her skinny black legs, flirting her tail. 'I saved you from the wolf! Wasn't I clever? Wasn't I good? What will you give me for saving you from the wolf? A little bit of cheese – have you got some? Or bacon? I like bacon when I can steal it! An egg – have you got an egg?'

Navvy reached into his coat. 'There's something here in my pocket you can have – '

Up ran Little Vixen to his feet, her nose sniffing for her reward, her treat –

And Navvy grabbed her by the tail, swung her up, swung her down, and smashed out her brains on a stone in the road.

Said Navvy – all together now, brothers – 'Old favours are soon forgotten!'

Navvy skinned Little Vixen and got a shilling for her pelt.

And this is truly what men are like, isn't it, brothers? You know it better than me. Cruel as wolves, cunning as apes – but two-faced as only men can be.

So come, my friends, steal my babbies' loaf that they were willing to share! Take their money, take my shirt – old favours are soon, soon forgotten!

The men had listened, mouths open, without a word to say. Now they drew breath and got, shaking, to their feet. Never, not for a second, did they take their eyes from the head lying on the old blue shirt, but they reached out to one another for something to lean on.

Then, leaving the shirt, leaving the money and most of the loaf – leaving, above all, the head – they took up their tools again and made off, around the clump of yellow-flowered broom and away across the hill. They showed black against the blue sky for a moment, and then they were gone.

First Born crawled over the grass to a lump of fallen bread, crumbled some of it and put it into the head's mouth. 'Which way now, Dadda?'

'I hear a stream running,' said the head. 'Find it, and follow it down the valley – it'll lead you to a big river. Then follow that.'

First Born nodded, and gently wrapped the head in his shirt again before tucking it into the crook of her arm. She stood, took her little brother's hand, and led him away down the hill to the valley and stream below.

3

It was a chill day, and the thick, feathery grey sky
hung close to the earth, making the world as dark
as dusk. The children were soaked through from
the last rainfall, and their flesh was marbled pink
and blue with cold. They plodded through long
grass that streaked their clothes with water,
beside a dirt track that was all puddles, and
stones, and small braided streams that trickled
into the larger one they followed. The cold, damp
wind blew through them, and over the open
heath beyond them, and into the grey sky beyond
that.

'I'm tired,' said the Little Un.

'I'm tired an' all,' said First Born, and trudged
on.

The little boy hung back on her hand. 'I want to
sit down.'

She yanked at his hand and tugged him on.
'Where you going to sit down? In a puddle? Come
on – it'll rain again in a minute.'

'I'm hungry.'

'So am I hungry.'

'I want to stop and have something to eat.'

'We'll stop when – '

The girl suddenly stopped herself and looked
about her, at the low-growing bilberries, bracken
and furze, at the soft dark clouds, full of rain. The

cold, wet wind blew across her cheek and through her wet clothes and made her shiver. There was no house in sight, and had not been all day. There was not so much as a wall or hedge to shelter behind.

The little boy let go of her hand and sat down at the side of the track, in the wet grass.

She held out her hand to him. 'Come on.'

He lay down, as if he would go to sleep.

First Born stooped over him. 'Little Un, we've got to go on.'

'Wh-y-y-y?'

'We can't stop here.'

'Why not?'

The girl put down her bundle, bent over her brother and tried to lift him to his feet. But he wriggled and kicked and held to the grass, and she couldn't lift him. With a thump and a small splash, she sat down beside him. 'Oh, let's stay here then,' she said. 'What's it matter? Maybe the rain'll pour and drown us and then nothing'll matter.'

Little Un sat up. 'Is there anything to eat?'

The girl reached for her bundle and unwound it. From its outer wrappings she produced the heel of a brown loaf, slightly damp from the rain. The other wrappings fell away as she put the bundle down, and revealed their father's head. Neither child glanced at it. First Born was tearing the bread in half, and Little Un was watching.

A gust of wind blew a wet slap of grass across the head's face, and it opened its eyes. A rain-drop fell into one and the head blinked. It looked out on a view of grey stone blackened by rain, wet ferns and grey sky. 'Where am we, me babbies?'

'Nowhere,' said the girl. The boy crawled through the mud to put a crumb of bread into the head's mouth.

'Hadn't we better get on and get somewhere?' asked the head, with its mouth full.

'Tired,' said the boy.

'We've been walking all day, and he's too tired,' said the girl. 'We've had enough and we don't want to walk anymore.'

'But your granny's waiting for you,' said the head.

'Don't care,' said the boy.

'It's too far,' said the girl. 'We could find a diggings, and Little Un could fetch and carry for the navvy-men, and I could wash their shirts. No more walking and walking in the rain.'

'But get up now and walk a bit further, babbies. It's going to be cold tonight. You've got to get out of the wind.'

'There is nowhere out of the wind,' said the girl.

'All right,' said the head, 'all right. You sit there in the puddles and eat your bit of bread, and I'll tell you a story to help it go down. How about – *East of the Sun, West of the Moon?*'

Harken then, and hark well – I won't say a word of it again if you miss it.

A long long time ago, and another hour before that, Mary lived with her mother in the diggings, cooking food and washing clothes for the navvy-men. But Mary thought she was for better than that. So, when she'd growed as tall as she was going to grow, she says to her mother, 'Mother, what am I going to do? How can I get what I want? How can I be happy?'

'Are you brave?' says her mother. 'Are you patient?'

'I'm brave and I'm patient,' says Mary. 'What do I do?'

'Tomorrow,' says her mother, 'it's Midsummer's Eve, when anything might happen, and wishes might come true. And if a brave wench went deep into the wood and waited by the big oak tree –'

'What?' says Mary.

'If she was patient enough to wait and wait –'

'I can be patient,' says Mary.

'Then along might come something and call her by name. And if she was brave enough to go with that thing, whatever it might be –'

'I'm brave enough!' says Mary.

'Then who knows what good might come of it?' says her mother.

So the next night, Midsummer's Eve, Mary left the diggings, and went off into the wood, where the flat pink dog-roses growed through the hawthorns, and the yellow honeysuckle growed through the hazels, and the air smelt of green leaves and sweet flowers. And she come to the big old oak, with all its green-gold leaves spread, and she sits down with her back against its trunk, and she waits.

One hour she waited, two hours she waited – patience, patience – and still it was light. It was midsummer. Wood pigeons cooed in the branches, squirrels ran along the ground and up the trees – but none of 'em called her by name. So three hours she waited, four hours she waited, and a fox went by, but didn't speak to her. And then the dark come, even on Midsummer's Eve, and the leaves of the oak gathered the darkness in. The birds sang off at the edges of the wood, and then fell quiet – oh, darkness and silence and honeysuckle scent in a midsummer wood.

The wench was tired and laid herself down to sleep under the oak, but then she heared a step on the forest floor, and a brushing of leaves and another step. And a voice said, 'Mary.'

Out she peered from under the oak's leaves and branches, and there she sees, shining in the dusk, the White Bear of England's woods. 'Climb on my back and go with me, Mary,' says the bear. 'Art brave enough for that?'

Mary was frit, and feared of the bear's long teeth and the bear's strong claws, but was she brave? She was brave. She come out from under the tree and clambered on the bear's broad back. Away the bear went with her, deep among the trees, deep into England's wood. Leaves brushed about her head, and she pulled down roses and woodbine. They come to dark streams running between steep green banks, under tunnels of hanging, leafy trees, and the bear carried her across dry. They went so deep into the wood that there was not a sound, but for the sound of leaves in the breeze; and then they came to a lost castle.

The castle's towers were like thick old trees, so growed with ivy they seemed built of dark green leaves. Hazel saplings and mushrooms guarded the gate, and wild roses had grown in through the little windows and flowered in the rooms inside. The bear carried Mary in through the gate to the courtyard, where blackberries hung from the walls. 'This is my castle,' says the bear, 'and here we'll live.'

It was a fine castle for a navvy-girl to live in. Every room smelt of green and flowers and forest; and there was a tang of forest in the cold water from the well. There was a great long table where Mary sat to eat a breakfast served her by ghosts – she couldn't see who carried the plates. And after she'd eaten, she went through a pointed door and found a bed, a real bed waiting for her, with pillows and covers and curtains, and garlands of honeysuckle. She lay down in it and slept the day away, and had never had such a soft sleep.

When she woke, it was night, and a new dress was spread out over the bed, and there was a fire lit in the grate, and a big bath set beside it, filled with warm water for her to wash. So she washed, and put on the new dress, and went out into the other room, where candles was burning and there was food on the table. 'This is a wonderful life,' she thought; and in through the door come the bear. He stood up on his hind legs, and he throwed off his skin like it was a coat, and under the skin was a lad, handsome lad, the best-looking lad ever you saw. He held out his hands to her and says, 'I'm a bear by day, and a man by night. Can you love me, Mary?'

She went into his arms and kissed him. 'Better a bear by day and a man by night than the other way around! I can love you.'

They sat close together at the long table and ate, and they talked until the candles burned out; and then they went through the pointed door into the other room and climbed into the bed together. But the next morning, at first light, the lad rose, pulled on his bearskin and was a bear again. When Mary woke, he was gone, out into the forest.

So every day Mary spent alone. She climbed to the tops of the towers, where there were little gardens of wild flowers growing between the stones, and she looked down on the tree-tops. She walked through all the castle rooms, and she went out into the forest herself; but she had no one to talk to until the bear came home at night, and threw off his bearskin and became her lad.

And she wished that he could be a lad all the time, so that they could always be together, and talk together, and so that she could always look at him. But every morning, at first light, he pulled on his bearskin and hid his own shape. Out into the forest he'd go and leave her lonely.

Time went by and time went on, until Mary had lived in the forest with Bearskin for a year, all but three days. And for a long time she'd been thinking, as she walked about the castle all alone, 'If he had no bearskin, he couldn't put it on. He'd have to stay with me, in his own shape, all day long.' And that night, after Bearskin was asleep, she slid out of bed and bundled the bearskin into the big fireplace. She rolled it up and heaved it into the fire, and she stoked the fire and tended it until the bearskin was burned into holes and charred bits. And she sat on by the fire until first light.

Then Bearskin woke and come looking for his pelt. He saw her smiling by the fire. He saw the ashes and the bits of burned hair and skin. And he cried out, 'Oh, Mary!' Up she jumped, all shaking with fear at what she'd done. 'Three more days!' he cried, 'three more days!' And then he vanished away.

The castle started to fall down. The window-ledges crumbled, the roof-tiles showered into the courtyard and crashed through the branches of the forest. The ivy pulled down the stones of the towers. From all around came a grumbling and a groaning as the stones shuddered apart.

'It's all over here,' said Mary. 'I must go.' And she walked away from the castle, and made her long weary way through the forest, pushing her way through close-growing trunks and tangling stems, crossing cold dark streams and wandering by many paths until she come to the navvy-camp, and there she wandered among the huts until she come upon her mother with her arms deep in a soapy washing-tub.

'I'm back, Mother!' says Mary, and her mother looked up, and then jumped up, and she hugged Mary with wet arms. And Mary sat down on the ground by the washing-tub and she told her mother everything that had happened to her. 'So he's gone, my lad of the bearskin, he's gone, he's gone, and left me lonely. How shall I find him? Where shall I look?'

'He's somewhere in this world or out of it,' says her mother. 'Search this whole world – walk to this world's end, and past there, and search out of it. You'll find him in the end.'

'All this world, and out of it,' said Mary. 'And how long will that take me?'

'Oh,' said her mother, splashing in the tub, 'until you've eaten a stone loaf, until you've worn out iron shoes, until you've climbed past Sun and Moon.'

'A stone loaf?'

'Only a stone loaf will last you so long.'

'Iron shoes?'

'Only iron shoes will last you so long.'

'Past Sun and Moon?'

'It's a long, long way you have to go.'

'Well,' said Mary, and sighed. She stood up, brushed off her skirt, kissed her mother and said, 'If I've so far to go, and so long to search, I'd better get started.'

And off she went on the frog and toad, tramp, tramp, tramp, to find a baker who could bake her a stone loaf. From village to town she tramped, from town to city, and up and down and round the streets she trudged, and asked at every baker's shop for a stone loaf. But there was only one baker who could bake stone into a loaf that could be eaten, and he said, 'My ovens will have to burn day and night to bake stone bread. It'll cost you dear. How will you pay me?'

Mary had no money. 'I'll work for you,' she said.

'You'll have to work seven years to pay me for a stone loaf,' says the baker.

'Then seven years I'll work,' says Mary.

And for seven years – seven long, long years – seven hot summers, seven cold winters – she worked for the baker, sweeping his floor, kindling his ovens, running about the streets to deliver the bread, mixing the flour and the yeast in the big wooden trough. But everything ends, even seven hard years of work, and at the end of it, she earned her stone loaf. And did she rest then? No. She tucked the loaf under her arm and went to the blacksmith.

'Make me a pair of iron shoes!' she said.

'Have you money to pay me? They'll cost you dear.'

'I'll work for you,' says Mary.

'For seven years? Seven years of work it'll take to pay for those shoes.'

'If seven years it must be, seven years it shall be. I must have those shoes,' Mary said.

So, for seven more long years – seven freezing winters, seven baking summers – Mary worked for the blacksmith, cooking his meals, sweeping his floors, washing his shirts, while the blacksmith did his own work and, between times, worked on the iron shoes.

Everything comes to an end, if you can wait, and the seven years ended, and Mary fastened the iron shoes on her feet, and set out to search the world – and out of it.

She walked, she limped, she nibbled her stone loaf, she lay down and slept; she rose up in the morning, ate stone for her breakfast, and walked on, whether it rained or whether it snowed, on she limped and fed herself on stone bread. Day after day, on and on she walked, further than anyone had ever walked before and eating what no one had eaten before, a stone loaf. And she didn't know which was the harder work, the walking or the eating. And though the end of the Earth was so far, the stone loaf was so hard that she'd only eaten half of it when she reached the Earth's end. It was dark and, through the dark, she saw the shining windows of a little house.

'Here might be a friendly face,' she thought. 'Here might be a warm place by the fire, and food a little softer than stone, and a dry bed.' And she knocked at the door of the house.

The door was opened by an old, old woman, whose wrinkled face was whiter than snow, and she stared when she saw Mary! She stared hard enough to stare a hole in a brick wall. 'My lover!' she said. 'Not a bird knows this place, the sun never touches us, and the winds never blow on us. So how have you found your way here?'

'I'm searching all the world and out of it,' says Mary, 'for my Bearskin. Can I come in and sit by your fire?'

'You look perished,' said the old woman, and drew her in by the hand. 'Sit you by the fire. Warm yourself outside and I'll get something to warm you inside. But you can only stay till it gets light, when my old man comes home. He'd pick your bones if he found you here.'

Mary sat by the fire, and the old woman brought her food and drink, and sat across the hearth from her, and they fell to talking. And Mary told the old woman all about her lad of the bearskin –

'The lad of the bearskin!' cried the old woman and clapped her hands together. 'Oh, was it you that burned the skin?'

'You know?' Mary said.

'Oh, I know all about Bearskin,' says the old woman. 'His mother died, and his father married a woman who was no woman but a trow, an imp, a bogy in disguise, and she had a trowish daughter with a nose five feet long – five feet long and scarlet at the tip! And she was set on marrying her daughter to our Bearskin, and when he wouldn't, she cursed him with a bear's shape by day – and the curse was never to be broken until a woman lived with him a whole year and never asked questions or tried to end his bear's shape!'

'Three more days!' said Mary. 'If I'd waited three more days, the spell would have been broken! Oh, I was brave, and I was patient, but I was three days short of patience enough! Where has he gone?'

'That I can't tell you, my lover,' said the old woman, 'but my old man might know.'

'Then I must stay and ask him! I must! I must find my Bearskin again!'

'All right, all right,' says the old woman. 'But we shall have to hide you until after he's had his dinner. My old man's always fearful hungry when he comes in, and he'll eat you for sure if he finds you!'

So they looked for a place for Mary to hide. There was a big cupboard beside the fireplace. 'When he comes, get in there,' said the old woman. 'You can peer through the keyhole and see him.'

And before long, they heard the old man tramping up the path, and Mary got into the cupboard, and the old woman shut the door on her. Mary put her eye to the keyhole and saw the old woman's old man come in.

He was the Moon. He carried a lantern in his hand, and his back was bent under a bundle of twigs that he dropped on the floor. His face was round and white as death, and he grumbled to himself, 'Oh, I'm tired! Up all night! Oh, I'm tired! Up all night!' But then he stopped, and sniffed, and said, 'I smell warm human flesh! Oh, wife, where is it, it makes me belly groan! Ooh, warm human blood, tasty, tasty!'

'Sit you down,' says his wife, 'take the weight off your poor old feet. Of course you smell human flesh – you've been over the world all night, sniffing it in! Here's your dinner, all hot from the oven.' And she banged a great bowl of hot steaming stew down on the table for him; and the Moon set to, with a big spoon, and was soon outside most of it.

The old woman sat at the table with him and talked. 'A young girl was here,' she says. 'I don't know how she found us. But she told me . . .' And the old woman told the Moon all that Mary had told her.

'Bearskin!' said the Moon, and shook his head, and sighed. 'A sad tale, wife, a sad, sad tale.'

And while she talked the old woman was up and down, filling the Moon's dish every time he emptied it, and cutting him slice after slice of bread, until he was so full, he couldn't have eaten so much as Mary's little finger. 'Now you can come out, Mary!' she said.

And Mary came out of the cupboard saying, 'Can you tell me where my Bearskin is?'

The Moon shook his head. 'I can't tell you where he is – but I'll send you on to my sister. She might know. But now I'm tired and I'm going to bed.'

And the Moon went to bed, where he slept all day. The old woman made up a bed on the hearth for Mary, and let her sleep a few hours, but woke her long before night came again. 'You'd better be on your way, my love,' she says. 'My old man always wakes up with his belly thinking his throat's cut, and if you're still here I might not be able to stop him gnawing on your bones.'

53

So Mary hurried to be off, and the old woman come out with her, to set her on the right road. In the garden by the house growed a tree, and silver nuts hung in its branches. The old woman picked one and give it to Mary. 'There you are, love. You take that along with you. Keep it safe now, and don't you ever crack it till you're at your greatest need.'

'I promise I won't,' says Mary, and puts it in her pocket.

'That's your way,' says the old woman, and points out a long steep road between dark banks of cloud and spiky, shining stars. 'Fare-you-well; take care.'

'Goodbye,' Mary said; and they hugged, and kissed, and Mary ran on up the road.

She ran, she walked, she trudged, she limped, she nibbled her stone loaf. She lay down and slept, she rose up and ate stone for her breakfast, and walked on, and the road was ever steeper until, one noon, she come to a little house.

'This must be Moon's sister's house,' she thought, and knocked at the door. An old man opened it and stared at her hard enough to bruise. 'No bird flies here,' he said. 'No river runs here, and no wind blows. However did you find us?'

'I'm searching the world and out of it,' says Mary. 'Moon sent me. Is this where his sister lives?'

'It is,' says the man, 'but she's always out all day. I'm her husband. Come in and tell me what you want.'

So Mary went into the house and sat by the fire, and the old man brought her food and drink and listened while she told of Bearskin, and her

54

travels, and of what Moon had said.

'My good wife might know something,' says the man, 'but she mustn't find you here. She always comes in so raging hungry, she'd swallow you down and you wouldn't touch the sides. But hide in there – that's the pantry.'

So when they heard the Goodwife coming home, Mary skipped behind the pantry door where she could hear everything and, by peering through the keyhole, see everything.

In come the Goodwife, banging open the door, and she was the Sun. She glowed, her long hair crackled, and she was beautiful. 'I smell warm human flesh!' she says. 'Oh! my mouth waters! Where is the mortal morsel?'

'You've been above the Earth all day,' says her husband. 'The smell's in your nose. Sit you down to the table, and I'll bring your dinner.' He served the Sun her dinner, piling her plate high, and talking all the time. 'A girl was here,' he says. 'Moon sent her.' And he told the Sun everything Mary had told him, and, while he talked, he filled and refilled Sun's plate, until she couldn't have eaten Mary's little toe.

'Poor girl, poor Bearskin,' says Sun, and shook her head. 'Sad, sad.' Her hair flared and crackled.

'You can come out now, Mary!' says the Sun's husband, and Mary come out of the pantry, asking,

'Can you tell me where to find my Bearskin?'

'Sorry,' says Sun. 'I don't know where he is. But I'll send you on to my brother, the Wind. He gets closer to the Earth than Moon or me, and he might know. But now I'm for my bed.'

The Sun's husband made Mary a bed on the

hearth, and she slept there all night, but early the next morning the old man woke her. 'You'd best get on your way,' he said. 'My wife always wakes so hungry, she'd have you on toast. I'll walk a little way with you, and set you on the right road.'

In a little garden by the house growed a nut tree, loaded down with golden nuts. The Sun's husband picked one and give it to Mary. 'Carry that with you, and never crack it till your need's greatest,' he said. Mary thanked him, and put the nut in her pocket, with the silver one the Moon's wife had given her.

'That's your way,' says the man, and he pointed out the long road that climbed up among clouds and stars. 'Farewell; take care.'

'Goodbye,' Mary says, and ran on up the road, but turned, once, to wave.

She ran, she walked, she trudged, and nibbled at the heel of her stone loaf, which was almost gone. She lay down and slept, she rose up and ate stone for her breakfast, and on she limped, in iron shoes that were wearing through. She'd passed the Moon and the Sun, but still she climbed, until she come to a little house.

'This must be Wind's house,' she said to herself, and she knocked at the door. It was answered by a woman whose mouth fell open wide enough to let a bird fly in.

'No bird flies here,' says Mary. 'Moon and Sun never shine here, no rivers run here – but still I've found you, and is this where the Wind lives?' The woman nodded. 'Sun and Moon sent me,' says Mary, 'to ask about Bearskin.'

'Come in, my love,' says the woman. 'Sit you by the fire. I'll get you something hot to eat and drink.'

So Mary sat by the fire and told the woman everything that had happened to her. 'We know of Bearskin,' says the woman, 'but where he is? That I can't say. I'll ask my husband when he comes – but we must hide you when he does – '

'Because he'll be hungry and would eat me?'

'You'd be in and down like a strawberry,' said the woman; and when the Wind was heard blowing up the path, she hid Mary at the bottom of a big laundry basket, and piled clothes on top of her.

'I'm all puffed out and hungry!' cried the Wind, throwing the door back against the wall. 'I smell a mortal! A small enough snack till me dinner's ready!'

'You've been blowing round the Earth all day and you've got the smell in your nose!' said the woman. 'Here's your dinner – sit to the table and eat up.' The North Wind pulled up his chair and started gobbling. His wife stood by and said, 'There was a girl here. She was asking about Bearskin . . .' And she told him everything Mary had told her, and every time his plate was almost empty, she filled it again, until he was so full that he couldn't have eaten the tip of Mary's nose.

'A sad story,' he says.

'Mary, you can come out now!' called the wife, and Mary climbed out of the laundry basket, asking,

'Can you tell me where to find my Bearskin?'

'I've blown to the south, to the east and the west,' says the Wind, 'but I've seen no sign of him . . . Still, tomorrow I shall blow to the North, and I'll look out for him. Sit down with us, my lass, and help my wife finish the stew. And keep all the bones –' He clattered a heap of bones from his own meal beside her plate. 'You might need them. As for me, I'm off to bed.'

The Wind's wife made Mary a bed on the hearth and she slept there nearly all night; but the woman woke her early in the morning. 'Up, up and follow me! We must get you hidden before my husband wakes up – he's always so hungry in the morning.'

In a little garden by the house growed a nut tree weighed down with nuts, and Mary crouched down behind the thick leaves and branches. The woman went back into the house, and soon Mary heard the Wind shouting for his breakfast, and for the mortal he could smell.

When the Wind come out of his house and rushed away to the North, Mary was able to go back inside, and help the woman with her chores, by way of repaying her. But that night she had to hide under the bed until the Wind had been fed full, before she dared come out and ask for news of Bearskin.

'I've seen him,' said the Wind. 'I blew rain and sleet around the towers of the Trow castle that stands high, high above all, East of the Sun and West of the Moon. And there was your Bearskin, in the courtyard, with trowie guards on either side of him. They treat him well, but he can't leave.'

'Oh, poor lad,' said the Wind's wife.

'The trows were in a tizzy, and I blowed through the windows of the kitchen and the hall, and listened to their talk. They're preparing for a great wedding feast.'

'Whose wedding?' asked Mary, and the Wind looked sadly at her.

'Bearskin's to be married to the trow princess in a week's time.'

'I must go!' cried Mary, jumping up, but the Wind said, 'Sit down, sit down, and help my wife finish the stew. Have you kept all those bones?'

'They're in my pocket.'

'Keep them safe – and take all these from the stew tonight. The trow castle is built in air – there's no way to it. But throw these bones in the air, and they'll make a ladder for you. Sleep well tonight. Tomorrow is soon enough to worry.'

So Mary went to her bed on the hearth, though the woman woke her early the next day, give her a nut from the tree, and walked with her a little way towards Trow Castle. Mary hugged her, and kissed her, and then ran on.

She ran, she walked, she trudged, she limped, and nibbled her stone loaf. She lay down and slept, she rose up and ate stone for her breakfast, and on she dragged herself, in iron shoes that were worn through. And she met a hungry little dog that skulked along the road, but whined and wagged his tail when he saw her. It was Moon's little dog, who'd got lost.

'Poor thing,' said Mary, and she took one of the bones from her pocket and threw it to him. Then on she went, tramp, tramp, tramp; and she came in sight of Trow Castle.

It was a castle in the air, high above her head, out of reach. Its tall towers rose up, through the darkness, its turrets above the stars. Candlelight glimmered from the narrow windows, and laughter drifted down from them to Mary, but there was no way up to the castle, no road, no track, no ground to carry a track. Nothing but air, stars and darkness.

Mary thought she'd weep, after all her hard journeying, after all her work, to come to the very place where her lad was, and not be able to reach him. But then she remembered the bones in her pocket, and took them out in handfuls and threw them in the air. Up they flew, they whirled, they fell – and joined together in a thin white ladder that reached from where she stood to the castle.

Not many would have the nerve to climb that ladder of rickety, trembling bones to a castle that stood on air – but Mary had worked for the stone loaf, she'd worked for the iron shoes, she'd climbed past Moon and Sun, and she wouldn't turn back now. She set hand to the ladder, she set foot to it, and she climbed.

Up and up and up – she looked down through the ladder, through miles of air and darkness, to the brightness of the sun and the gleam of the moon, and the Earth like a dish far below her. The ladder juddered, it clacked and clattered and shook beneath her, but up she climbed and up until – but she still couldn't reach the castle. Remember the bone she chucked to the dog? Now the ladder was short of a bone. What was she to do, just one bone away from the castle? Where was she to get another bone?

From her belt she took her sharp knife, and with one good chop she chopped off her little finger and put it in place of the last bone. And up the ladder she scrambled to the gate of Trow Castle.

As the drops of her blood fell all the way down

to Earth, Mary knocked at the gate, and knocked, and shouted, 'Let me in, let me in! I can carry, I can bake, I can fetch, I can scrub, I can wash, I can sew, I can *work*!'

The gate was opened and the trows let her in, and they gave her work in the kitchen, scrubbing the greasy pots, sweeping the ashes, grinding bones into flour for the trows' bread – but she was careful not to eat a crumb of their bread herself because she knew that those who eat a trow's food become trows themselves. She fed herself on the very last of her stone loaf.

Every chance she got, she left her work and sneaked into the trows' feasting-hall and there, in the yellow blaze of candles, seated at the high table, she saw the trowie princess with her five-foot nose bobbing above the plates and, beside her, the best-looking lad in the world, Mary's own lad, the lad of the white bearskin.

'Grind faster,' said the trows in the kitchens. 'Grind more bone-flour. We need barrels of it for the wedding feast.' So she knew that her lad and the trow weren't married yet.

Mary tried and tried to get a chance to talk with the lad, but he was always hunting with the trows, or shut up in some little room with the trow princess. A grubby kitchen-maid – and one who wasn't even a trow – couldn't get near him.

Here am I, she thought, beyond the end of the world. I see my lad every day, but he doesn't see me and I can't speak a word to him. Will my need ever be greater? And she thought not.

So she went into the yard and stood under the window of the trow princess. 'Princess!' she called, 'Princess!' And first the princess's nose poked over the sill, and then the princess's head. 'Princess, I want to talk with the man you're going to marry!'

'Get back to your work,' said the trow.

'Please, let me spend just one night with him!'

'Back to your greasy pots!' And the trow princess pulled her head in.

From her pocket Mary took the silver nut from the Moon's tree, and played throw and catch with it. It shone as it flew up, it sparkled as it fell down, and it caught the eye of the trow princess.

Out of the window come her head again and her eyes narrowed, and her long nose twitched. 'I want that!' she said.

'Pay for it!' said Mary.

'What's the price?'

'One night with the lad you're going to marry!'

'Too much!' said the trow.

But Mary cracked the nut against the wall, and from inside it there spilled out a dress made of silver thread and stitched with moonstones, that glimmered and shimmered like moonlight itself. The trow princess leaned far out of the window to see it, and she sighed as she thought of herself in that silver dress. She wanted it.

'One night! No more than one night!' And down come the trow from her tower to take the silver nut-shell, and the beautiful silver dress.

She cheated though, the trow. That night, before the lad went to bed, she give him a drink to make him sleep, and when Mary was let into his room, she couldn't wake him. She called to him, she touched him, she shook him, but he slept on. She sat by his bed, and she sang:

Seven, seven years I worked for thee,
A loaf of stone I gnawed for thee,
I wore through iron shoes for thee,
My finger, my finger I chopped for thee,
And won't you waken and turn to me!

But day come and the lad still slept, and Mary went back to the kitchens to grind bones to flour. But she still had the nut from the Sun's tree and the nut from the Wind's tree.

So the next day she sneaked away from the kitchen and went to stand under the trow princess's window. From her pocket she took the golden nut from the Sun's tree, and she tossed it in the air and caught it. It glittered as it flew up and flashed as it fell down, and the trow princess stuck her nose out of the window, and her head after it, and said, 'What do you want for that?'

'A night with the lad you're going to marry!'

'Too much!'

Mary cracked the nut against the wall, and from it spilled a dress made all of golden thread, sewn with citrine and topaz, that flashed and glared like the sun itself. And the trow princess looked down and sighed as she thought of herself in that dress. She wanted it.

'One night!' said the princess, and down she come from her tower to claim her golden nutshell and her golden dress.

But what's worked once will maybe work again, so again she give the lad a drink to make him sleep, and when Mary was let into his room, he wouldn't wake for anything she could say or do, not even when she sang:

Seven, seven years I worked for thee,
A loaf of stone I gnawed for thee,
I wore through iron shoes for thee,
My finger, my finger I chopped for thee,
And won't you waken and turn to me!

Day come, and still the lad slept, and Mary had to go back to the kitchen, to make bone broth and grind bone flour.

But it happened that day, that the lad went hunting with a party of trows, and one of them said to him, 'What is this singing and sighing, this weeping and moaning from your room these two nights past?'

The lad didn't know what was meant, because he'd slept so deep the two nights, and hadn't heard anything. And he was puzzled.

Now Mary, soon as she could, took the last of her treasures, the Wind's nut, and went to stand under the trow princess's window. She tossed the nut up, and it sparkled; down it fell into her hands, shining. Out of the window came the five-foot nose of the trow princess, and then the princess's head, and she said, 'What do you want for that?'

'Another night with the lad you're going to marry!'

'Too much!'

Mary cracked the nut against the wall, and from it spilled a dress made all of feathers, all soft and shining: jay-blue, kingfisher-green, chaffinch-pink, robin-red . . .

'One night!' said the trow princess, and come down to seize the feather-dress and carry it away. But again she meant to cheat, and give the lad a drink to make him sleep. She wasn't to know that the lad remembered what he'd been told about the sighing and singing in his room, and poured the drink out of his window to splash, far, far below, on the Earth. He lay down without having drunk it. But he went to sleep.

Mary was let into his room, and she called to him, and she touched him, but he was too deep asleep to hear her. Then she sat down on the bed and sang:

> Seven, seven years I worked for thee,
> A loaf of stone I gnawed for thee,
> I wore through iron shoes for thee,
> My finger, my finger I chopped for thee,
> And won't you waken and turn to me!

And that woke him. He sat up in bed and looked at her, and put his arms round her and said, 'Oh, Mary, I remember thee.'

And she said, 'I was three days short of the patience to break the curse, but seven patient years I worked for the baker, and seven patient years I worked for the smith, and far I've walked and high I've climbed, and is that enough?'

It was. The Trow castle fell down about the trows, and let in the western sunlight to kill them. Mary and her lad clambered back down her ladder of bones, and ran back down the long road to Earth, and walked back to their own castle in the forest; and there they lived forever happy, because Mary was brave, and Mary was patient, and had knowed she was for better than washing navvy-men's dirty shirts, me babby, she knowed she was for better than washing navvy-men's dirty shirts.

The story was done, the last of the damp bread had been eaten, and the dampness in the air had turned to a drizzle, which had turned to rain. The head lay in its sodden wrappings, its dark hair weighed down with water and sending streams pouring down its face into its wet beard. The children were no less wet, and could feel the rainwater running over their skin under their clothes.

'Up!' said the girl, and climbed to her feet. She wrapped the head in its wet shirt, and tucked it under her arm. 'Up!' she said again to the boy, holding out her hand. 'We've got to follow this stream down to the big river.'

The boy took hold of her hand and allowed her to pull him to his feet. Together they splashed off through the brown stream that poured along the muddy track.

'We'll walk,' said the girl, 'to the end of the earth, where Granny lives.'

'Will we have a stone loaf to eat?'

'No, we'll have a stone cake with pebbles for currants.'

'And stone pancakes?'

'And stone pancakes, and stone pikelets with mud for butter – so we'll never need to go hungry!'

And before full dark they found a stone-walled pen, built for ewes and their lambs, and they were able to sit down together in a corner. They were cold, and hungry again, and uncomfortable in their wet clothes, but they were out of the wind, which would have killed them if they hadn't walked on and found shelter.

4

In the shade of a tree, but close enough to the
river to see the swell of dark water, sat a monk.
The leaves above him were shaken by the breeze
that cooled the heat, and the light came down
through them and spattered him with green and
gold twinklings. Standing, he would have been
an unusually tall man. Even sitting, with his
broad shoulders and back slumped forward in a
great curve, he could be seen to be big. His long,
bare, hairy legs stuck out at the hem of his grey
habit, and on his big feet were big brown sandals. His big hands were clasped around his
drawn-up knees.

He sat looking about him at everything – at the
little flotillas of ducks and moorhens that skim-
med so fast and silently over the water, making
silver 'v's before them; at the slow cows in the
field, wandering from sun to tree-shade; at the
leaves above him waving and making patterns
against the bright sky. His face was broad and
plain, not in any way handsome, but pleasant,
friendly and interested. The remains of a small
loaf, a lump of cheese and an open clasp-knife
lay in the grass beside him. To his other side was
a curious metal box, bound with strips of metal,
studded with coloured stones, and inlaid with
engraved panels.

When he saw two children coming towards him along the riverbank, he watched them with even more attention than he had given to the water birds. They were a rough looking pair, with great clumps of uncut, uncombed dark hair, and clothes that were all crumpled and stained from having been soaked, and dried, and slept in, and soaked again. The way the bigger child hugged a bundle under one arm, gripped the younger by the hand, and stumped along through the meadow grass without ever looking about at what was to be seen, amused him. So, when the children came nearer, the man unclasped his hands, leaned his chin in one and called out, 'Good day to you, little ones!'

First Born stopped and stood stiff and wary, holding her brother's hand and looking fixedly at the stranger.

'You look as if you've been walking a while,' said the man. He spread one large hand towards the bread and cheese in the grass. 'Hungry, are you?'

The smaller child said, 'Ar!' in the deep voice of a small boy with a cold, and took a step forward. But his sister wouldn't let go of his hand and held him back.

The man smiled and got to his feet. The children gaped at him. He was higher up the bank than them, and that, and his own height, made him a giant and startled them. And he wore a long dress. He turned his back on them and took three or four long strides higher up the bank, and threw himself down again on the soft, thick grass, lying at his full, long length, and propping himself up on one elbow. Behind him, on the flattened grass, he had left his bread and cheese, and his useful knife; and the strange round box, its dull silver and stones and gilding glittering in the green grass, as the leaf-broken light shifted over it.

'Help yourselves,' said the big man. 'I've eaten all I want.'

The girl still watched the man, but allowed the boy to tug her a little closer to the food. When the monk didn't move, they went right to it, and the boy dropped down in the grass. He tore the bread in half, and passed half up to his sister, who still stood, keeping watch. The man smiled at her. When he stopped looking at her, and began to watch the birds on the river again, the girl knelt down and reached for the knife and cheese. But she kept an eye on the man, ready to jump up and run.

The boy had been looking at the silver, gilded box. He poked its hard side with a finger. 'What's that?'

The man looked round. 'A reliquary.'

'What's one of them?'

'A reliquary . . . is for keeping a relic in.'

The boy chewed hard on stale bread. 'What's a relic?'

The man rolled on his hip and sat up, with his knees apart and the soles of his sandals together. 'A relic is . . . part of a saint that we keep in memory of the saint, and as a holy object.'

'What's a saint?'

The big man laughed, drew up his knees and hugged them. 'Well now, a saint is a very good, holy person, who loves God and is loved by God, and can perform miracles.'

The boy looked at his sister, who shrugged. 'What's a miracle?' he asked.

'You are a little heathen,' said the man.

'What's a heathen?'

'*You* are a heathen because you know nothing of God – and a miracle is – a miracle – I don't know how to tell you. But in that box is the head of Saint Unencumbere, and many's the miracle that head's performed. People have come limping to her shrine, and have pranced away, leaping and capering. The blind have seen again, the dumb have spoken, the deaf have heard, the constipated been opened and the loose closed. That's the power of a prayer to Saint Unencumbere.'

The boy reached out and tried to open the box, but it was locked. 'Can I see her?'

'Better not. She isn't pretty.'

'Have you seen her?'

The big man nodded. 'She's not so bad when you're used to her. Many's the time,' he said proudly, 'that I've combed out her beard.'

Both the children laughed, and the monk looked shocked.

'A woman with a beard!' said the girl.

'A beautiful beard she has! It's a sign of her holiness – listen. No, listen! I'll tell you. Unencumbere was a beautiful princess, a most beautiful one – but her Daddy, the King, he was a pagan – '

'What's a pagan?' asked the boy.

'One like you, who's never heard of Jesus Christ. So her Daddy was a pagan, but she heard the Word, and she became a good Christian. But then her Daddy, the King – '

'The pagan,' said the boy.

'The pagan – he wanted her to marry another pagan King. He insisted! Said he would kill her if she didn't. So she prayed to Our Lord, and in answer to her prayers, Our Lord made a beard grow on her chin overnight – it isn't funny!'

The monk watched sternly until both the children had managed to stop laughing – or, at least, to stop laughing so much. 'You don't deserve to hear the rest,' he said. 'Little heathens you are, both!'

'Oh, tell us the rest,' said the girl.

'Go on,' said the boy. 'Tell us the rest.'

'Well . . . When the pagan King saw she had a beard, he didn't want to marry her any more. Called the wedding off! But her Daddy said, "Aha! Since you love your Jesus Christ so much, you can go the same way!" And he had her crucified.'

'What's crucified?' the boy asked.

'Oh, I'm no match for your ignorance,' said the monk. 'But let me tell you that she's a great saint. If you want to die in peace, call on Saint Unencumbere. If you can't sleep, call on Saint Unencumbere. And if you're a woman with a bad husband, then call on Saint Unencumbere and she'll unencumber you. Also she helps men with scanty beards grow thick ones.'

'And that's her head you have in the box?' the girl asked. 'Where are you taking her?'

'Ah.' The big man shuffled his big feet through the grass. 'That's a sad story and a long story. She was the treasure of our monastery – the only treasure we've had, these last years. That wasn't always so. In the old days, when

71

Saint Unencumbere spoke and performed so many miracles, we had lines of pilgrims at our doors, squabbling and shoving and pushing to get in first, and bringing us gifts. But the saint hasn't said a word now for more than a hundred years, and she doesn't listen to prayers so often either. So our house is closing, and I'm sent to take the saint to her new home in France, where they have livelier bits of livelier saints, and poor old Saint Unencumbere'll be put away in her reliquary, and I doubt she'll ever be looked at or prayed to again. She'll be forgotten.'

The children were quiet after this, and sat looking at each other as they ate the last of the bread and cheese. The monk watched them and smiled, thinking that they hadn't understood the half of what he'd said – which was quite true.

But when the last of the food had been eaten, the girl said, 'Do you want to see our head?'

'Your head?'

'We've got a head an' all – but we wouldn't keep him in a tin.'

'We've got him wrapped in his old shirt,' said the boy.

The girl had unslung a bundle from her back, and was unwrapping it. Puzzled by their words, the monk watched closely – and couldn't help but give a start when the head was revealed. It lay on its cheek with its eyes closed, and its mouth in a lazy half-smile, seeming to be asleep, so freshly coloured was it. It was much less ugly than the head of Saint Unencumbere, and the fact that it had no body seemed more odd than horrible.

'How did you come by that?'

'It's our dad,' said the girl, and the boy reached over and tugged a lock of the head's dark, faintly greyed hair. The head's eyes opened slowly; and then its mouth stretched in a yawn so wide that its eyes were closed again.

The monk gave another little start – but, after all, Saint Unencumbere's head had once spoken, he devoutly believed. He crossed himself.

'Wake up, Dad!' said the boy, lying down with his own head in the grass, so he could look into his father's face. 'Here's a man's got another like you locked up in a box!'

'Another like me?' said the head. Its voice rasped, as if it had a sore throat. 'There is no other like me!'

'There is, in that box,' said the girl, and she lifted the head a little so that it could see the box. 'He's got a head in there that talks and works magic – he said so!'

The woken head squinted against the bright sunlight, and saw the casket glinting in the grass. 'Open it!' he said. 'Let's have a look!'

The big monk came crawling down the grassy bank towards them. Kneeling beside the casket, he took hold of a chain around his neck and hauled up, from inside his robe, a key. He unlocked the casket and tipped back its lid. Inside was a dandelion-puff of fine, white hair and, at the centre of the puff, a small round thing, brown and shrivelled. Its wrinkled brown lids were closed over bulging eyes, its face was hollow under its sharp cheekbones, and its drawn-back lips showed its long yellow teeth. The cloud of white hair grew, in quantities,

73

from the crown of its head, and from its cheeks and chin.

'He don't look too well,' said Linnet. 'What's up with him?'

'Her, her,' whispered the girl. 'It's a woman, Dad.'

'*Her*? Well, what's up with her, then?'

'Nothing, sir,' said the monk. 'Except that she's been separated from her body for hundreds of years.'

'Poor old soul,' said Linnet.

The girl pointed to the monk. 'He said her spoke.'

'Indeed she did speak,' said the monk. 'We have the word of many honest, holy men for that – but it was a long time ago, in an age of greater faith. She used to speak with the pilgrims that came to her shrine, give them advice, and bless them and pray with them. People used to come regular, just to have a chat about their troubles with Saint Unencumbere. It was a great comfort to the flock. But Saint Unencumbere hasn't said a word now – oh, since a time before anyone alive can remember.'

'All those pilgrims, coming with their complaints,' said Linnet. 'Enough to make anybody fall into a gloom. All tramping there, from all the country round, to tell her their troubles, and her having to lie there and listen. Poor old soul. Tell you what – there's not a lot I can do, being only a head meself – but I can tell a story. I'll tell her a story to cheer her up.'

The children laughed, and lay down in the grass, ready to listen. But the monk's hands hovered towards the reliquary, as if he would close and lock the box again. 'What kind of a story?'

'A good story,' said Linnet. 'A fine story.'

'A story fit for a saint?'

'A story fit for anybody with ears on the sides of their heads. The story of – *The Hag and the Navvy.*'

'"The Hag and the Navvy",' the monk muttered worriedly. 'I'm not sure about this . . .'

'Settle down,' said Linnet. 'Arrange your feet. Clear your throats, shift your bums and wipe your noses, 'cos here we go –'

There was a young navvy, and he was a pretty lad, taller than a door and strong as a horse. He could work all day and dance all night, and he wasn't much for staying in one place, but would pack up his gear and move on if he heard of a ganger paying half-a-penny more at another diggings.

So there he was, swinging along on the tramp with his tools on his back; and the sun shining, just like it is today, and the birds was yelling, and the river was running past faster than he could walk. And this handsome young navvy meets with an old woman, a real hag, and she was staggering along with a load of sticks and grass on her back that was almost too much for her. Her knees was bent under it, and first to one side of the road she'd go, nearly falling over, and then back the other way, and so backwards and forwards, tottering and nearly falling all the while.

But what a hag, what an ugly hag! I'll tell you how ugly she was. Her hair was grey as fog, and so greasy, it seemed soaking wet: it hung in greasy strings. Her skin was as greasy and grey as her hair, like greasy grey porridge it was. And her eyes – her eyes were red with blood, and had crusts of yellow matter at the corner; and the lower lids sagged low to show the wet red linings ... And so crossed were her eyes that she could only see the big lumpy end of her own puffy red nose ... And from her nose hung ropes of thick yellow snot down to her chest. She only had three yellow teeth, and her lips wouldn't close over 'em, and so she drooled ...

'This is not a nice story,' said the monk.

... And the smell of her! The smell that rolled off her as she came –

'Please – do we have to hear of the smell?' asked the monk.

The smell would choke a fox. It would curdle a cesspit. It would make a stone crumble. It hit our young navvy like a punch in the face and made him reel on his feet!

'Oh, enough!' said the monk.

It was nearly enough to finish our lad. But he turned his head aside and got a breath of fresh air, and then he said, 'What are you doing here, all by yourself, my young beauty? Don't look at me now, don't bat those eyelashes, or you'll break my heart!'

'Oh, so you teach these children to mock the ill-favoured!' said the monk. 'It's a wicked, idle tale!'

That's what the young navvy said to the old hag. But what did she say to him? 'Oh,' she says, 'when you have a straight, strong young back, and straight, strong young legs, it's very pleasant to stand and laugh at the old and bent. When you've young limbs without an ache in them, it's very amusing to laugh at me, who's pain in every inch of me, pain in the morning and pain all day, and pain when I crawl into bed at night. When you're young and beautiful, it's great fun, I daresay, to jeer at some poor ugly soul who's never known what it was to be pretty and please folk's eyes. Well, laugh away! Laugh all you like! There's nothing I can do to stop you.'

'That made the young navvy ashamed. 'Grandmother, I'm sorry,' he says. 'Let me make it up to you. Let me carry your load.'

'Ah,' said the monk, wriggling to be comfortable in the grass. 'This is a little better.'

'Get on your way,' says the old hag. 'You couldn't carry me load – I'm carrying it home, and that's an hour's walk.'

'An hour's walk!' says the navvy. I'd run that! Give me your load here.'

'I tell you, you couldn't carry it,' says the old hag. 'I've carried it every day of my life. I'm used to the weight, I'm used to the pains. If I was struck dead, I wouldn't stop until I reached home and laid the load down. But you – 'Oh, fine looks, fine talk – but you couldn't carry my load a yard!'

Now the young navvy started to be angry. 'Give it here!' he says. 'Let me show you how far I can carry it!'

'Right,' says the old hag, and she swung the load down from her own back and swung it up on to his.

Well, the navvy felt as if his back was broke! He'd never had a heavier weight laid on it. It bent him over, it buckled his knees, it made the sweat burst out of him. 'Oh, look, look!' the old woman shouts, and for all her aches and pains, she danced in the road. 'The strong young man can't carry what an old woman can carry, he can't carry what an old woman can carry!'

'I can, look, I can!' the navvy gasps, and he struggled on along the road, his knees wavering under him, and seeming ready to fall on the hard road in a heap at any moment. Well, he managed until the road went up a hill, that got steeper and steeper. The navvy's heart hammered inside him, his legs weakened, his head throbbed and seemed like to burst, the sweat poured off him. He thought he was going to die.

'I've got to have a rest, Gran!' he says.

'No!' she said, 'Oh, no! Keep going!'

The navvy took no notice, and tried to throw the load off his back, but he could no more throw it off than he could his own skin. It made him mad – and afraid – to hear the old hag laugh.

'Get on,' she says, 'get on – carry it home for me, and maybe I'll give you a little something for yourself. But there must be no stopping to rest.'

So the navvy struggled on, with each step

making him think his heart'd burst, and the sweat running off him like water runs out of a pump. And just when he could see the top of the hill and thought the worst was over, the old woman jumps up on his back, on top of the load! And thin and scrawny though she was, she weighed as much as a bullock.

Too much! Down on the hard, sharp stones crashed the navvy on his poor knees. The old woman laughed and thrashed him with nettles she'd cut from the hedge. 'On! On!' she said. 'The exercise'll make you stronger yet! It'll make stopping sweeter!' And on the navvy had to crawl, with his back feeling that it would crack in two. And the old hag sat on his shoulders, with the streams of her snot and her dribble pouring down his back and muddying the road behind them –'

'Oh, horrible!' said the monk. 'He deserved something for the way he spoke to the old woman, but this is torture and sheer nastiness! Don't you know any nicer stories?'

'Ssh!' said the girl fiercely, which made the monk stare, but silently.

Now the navvy had been wrinkling his nose at a smell even worse than the smell of the old hag on his back, and just at the top of the hill they met with a goose-girl, and her flock of geese. It was the goose-girl who smelled so bad. Her feet were bare, and she had great horny toe-nails that chipped lumps out of the hard road as she walked.

'Hello mother!' says the goose-girl.

'Hello sweetheart!' says the old hag. 'Say hello

79

to this nice young man who's helped me home.'

So the goose-girl bends over and says 'hello' to the navvy; and she was worse looking than her mother. She was snaggle-toothed, big-nosed, small-eyed, no-chinned and scraggy, scrawny, skinny as a twig.

'Hop up, me girl!' says the old hag. 'Why walk when you can ride?'

The navvy had no breath to say no, and up on his back the goose-girl jumped, and she weighed more than her mother. 'On! On! said the old hag, and beat him with her bunch of nettles, and on he had to drag himself, on up the hill with all the white geese clustering, wobbling and honking around him.

Just over the top of the hill was a little house, with a bench outside the door, and an apple tree growing near it, and a pool under the tree. 'Here we are,' says the old woman. 'It hasn't been so far, has it? And it hasn't been so hard, what with us cracking jokes to while away the time. Crawl over to that bench, and you can lie down and have a rest.'

So the navvy crawled and dragged himself off the road, past the pool and the apple tree, and over the grass to the house and the bench by its door. There the goose-girl and the old hag jumped down, and pulled the load off his back, and the navvy lay flat in the grass, closed his eyes, gasped for breath, and thought he would never move again.

The two hags left him lying there while they dragged the load into the house. When the old hag came out again, she was carrying a cup of milk and a plate of stew. 'There's the little something for yourself,' she said. He could hardly sit up for long enough to eat and drink, but he licked both plate and bowl clean, and lay down again. And he was so worn out, he fell asleep.

'Is that the end?' the monk asked.
'No!' said Little Un.

When he woke, the sun had gone down, and the white moon and the white stars had come out in a black sky. He was still lying in the soft grass outside the cottage, but now he was cold – and he could hear singing. Someone – a woman – was singing quietly.

He pushed himself up on his elbow and peered through the darkness. He could see something moving – someone was walking across the grass to the pool by the apple tree. Whoever it was moved with a stump and a stomp and a stagger – it was the young hag, the ugly goose-girl, and she was singing to herself, with a sound like a creaky gate.

Then the moon come from behind a cloud, and by its light the navvy saw the goose-girl taking off her clothes – '

'I want you to stop this story now!' cried the monk.

But when she had taken off all her clothes, she didn't stop there –

'Remember there are children listening!'

No, she took off her skin too. From the top of her head down, she peeled it off. Off came her grey, greasy hair; off her came her face; off came the skin covering her arms and body, off came the skin covering her legs. And underneath – '

'Was she a bony skelington?' asked Little Un.
'No.'
'Was she – ?' First Born pulled a face. 'All raw meat?'
'No.'
'Putting such ideas into their heads,' said the monk. 'I wish to say, here and now, that I don't approve.'
'Underneath,' said Linnet, 'the goose-girl had another skin. When she took off the ugly one, she stepped out of it as a smooth young girl – '
'With not a stitch on her!' said the monk.

Not a stitch. She stood as straight and as slim as a young birch, and every curve of her body was as firm and plump as a young pig. Her dark hair hung down her back and its curls were lifted by every little breeze. She stepped from foot to foot as she went across the grass to the pool, so lovely as she moved that the young navvy got up from where he was lying without even knowing he had. The sight of that lovely young girl pulled him along as a hook pulls along a fish. Across the grass he crept, closer and closer – what, Brother?'

'Nothing!' said the monk. 'Go on.'

'Well, since you ask me . . . Closer and closer he crept, and watched as the lovely girl stepped into the pool, and as she knelt and washed the cold water over her shoulders. Could he just see her face? Could he just see if her face was as lovely as the rest of her! But her back was to him, and he could only see her long, dark hair floating on the water.

So then he thinks to himself that if he got hold of that haggish skin she'd been wearing – and hid it – or, better still, took it into the cottage and burned it on the fire – she would never be able to put it on again, and she would always be beautiful – '

'Such impure thoughts he's having!' said the monk, rocking backwards and forwards. 'Go on!'

He looked around, and there he sees it, lying on the grass, a dark patch in the moonlight – the hag-skin. And he crept away from the pool, making only a little rustling in the grass, such as the breeze might make, and he reached the hag-skin and was just picking it up – when a voice said, 'You creeping, sneaking, dirty, peeping cheating little toe-rag.' It was the old hag, and she was watching him with her hands on her hips. 'Spying on my daughter!' she said, and pointed at him. 'Be blind!'

And the navvy was struck blind. The sight went from his eyes. The moon, the stars, the apple tree, the pool, the lovely girl, the old hag – he could see none of them, no more than if he had his head in a sack. He might have had pebbles for eyes, for all he could see.

Now he was frightened, the navvy, and turned himself around and hurried away from the pool, though he couldn't see anything of where he was going. He walked over grass, and over rocky paths. He felt in front of him with his hands and felt nothing. He stumbled on banks, and fell over tussocks, blundered into hedges and scratched his face. But whenever he fell, he got up again and went on, because he was scared, and because he couldn't believe that he was blind, even though he couldn't see.

In the end, he fell into a clump of thorn bushes, and there he stuck. He couldn't get out, because he couldn't see how the thorny branches had tangled in his clothes, he couldn't untangle them, and every time he moved the thorns scratched and pricked him. So he sat there, in the thorns, and cried because he thought he'd never get out.

But then he heard a voice saying to him, 'Never mind, never mind.' It was the ugly goose-girl, who had come to find him. He felt her fingers unfastening the thorny branches from his clothes, and then she took both his hands in hers, and led him out of the bushes. 'Here,' she said, and put something into his hand. 'I have to get back before mother finds I'm gone, but this is for you, I made it.'

'What is it?' the navvy asked, turning the thing over in his hand. It felt smooth and hard.

'It's a box; it's full of ointment – now I must go!' And he heard her bare feet running away over the grass.

The navvy sat down on the ground and fiddled with the little box until he got the lid off. He sniffed the ointment, and it smelt of thyme. He dipped his fingers into it, and it was cold and smooth – and he rubbed it on his arm, where it was scratched and sore. Straight away, the cuts and scratches felt better. So he put it on more places where the thorns had scratched him, and they felt so much better that he dipped his finger in the ointment and rubbed it on his eyes.

'And did it make his eyes better?' asked the monk.

The ointment made his eyes sting and water, but when he blinked the water away, he saw dim shapes of trees, as if through a fog. And then, when he blinked more, the colours came back and the shapes got clearer – and he could see even better than before.

'The Lord be praised.'
'Not any lord, brother – the goose-girl.'
The monk opened his mouth to say something to that, but First Born said, 'Oh, get on with the story!' And Little Un said, 'Ar – the story, get on with it!'

Well, there our navvy was, sitting in the grass by the thorn bushes, looking around at the sky and the trees and the light with his new eyes – and then he looked down at the box of ointment in his hand – and it wasn't a box, but a locket. A battered old silver locket, engraved with roses, with a loop for a chain to go through.

And he sits there a bit longer and thinks of the girl who gave it to him – the ugly goose-girl, who was really a beauty – 'And kind too,' he thinks. 'And her living with that wicked old woman and frightened to death of her!' So up he gets and he sets off to find the cottage again, and see if he can't get the girl away from the old hag.

But no matter how he walks or where he walks, no matter how many times he goes back over the same ground, no matter how long he stands still and thinks, no matter who he asks for directions, he can't find a sign of that cottage, or get word of it, or see anything he recognizes. So, in the end, he has to give up and go on his way.

'Anyway, I've got an ointment that makes the blind see,' he says to himself. 'That should be worth a bit! Even the locket might fetch a penny or two.' And off he goes on the tramp, tramp, tramp.

'Is that the end?' asked the monk.

'Oh, shut up!' First Born said.

The navvy thought he would go to a big city to try and sell his ointment, because he'd get a better price there. So off he tramped to the King's city – but plenty happened on the way. First, he come across a man who'd cut himself on a scythe, a real bad cut. But a smear of the ointment from the locket made the cut close up and scab over, and another touch healed it!

And then, in another place, the navvy went into a pub and found the people talking about a little girl who was dying. 'Take me to her!' said the navvy, and they did, and though the little girl was properly sick and in her last hours, a smear of the ointment on her lips had her sitting up and asking for food in the time it takes to draw a long breath.

After that the navvy found people had heard of him before he got to them, and were waiting for him. 'Are you the man with the ointment?' they'd say, and they'd drag him off to a house where somebody was sick or dying. With a touch of his ointment he healed ulcers and sores, he straightened twisted fingers and backs, he took away pain, made hair grow again and cured all kinds of ills. And however much ointment he used, there always seemed to be as much as before left in the little locket.

So when he got to the big city, crowds were waiting for him, and everybody in the crowd shouting out that he should come with them first. But there was a carriage waiting, with six big black horses harnessed to it, and men got down from the carriage and grabbed the navvy and shoved him inside, closed the doors, whipped up those black horses and drove away before the navvy could speak to anyone.

'A big carriage? Black horses?' said the monk. 'Is it the Devil?'

It wasn't the Devil; it was a rich man, getting in first to grab what the poor need more but can't buy, like the rich always do. The rich man was sitting there, in the carriage, and he said to the navvy, 'I want you to cure my wife with your ointment.'

'What's the matter with her?' asked the navvy.

'She's sad,' said the rich man. 'She lies in her bed and hardly eats, hardly drinks. She cares for nothing, and says she wants to die.'

'Poor woman,' said the navvy. 'How did she come to that?'

The rich man sighed and seemed sad. 'I'll tell you,' he said, as the horses pulled the carriage on through the streets, and they were jumped and jolted about inside. 'Many years ago, we weren't rich. No, we were so poor, we hadn't a piece of bread in the house, or a coin in money to buy any. We tried and tried to get work, but we couldn't – there were too many others looking for work. And our little girl – we had no food to give her, and we were watching her starve . . .' Tears started to run down the rich man's face. 'When we could get food, we gave it to her, but that made us weak, and the weak don't find work . . . What could we do? If we starved ourselves, then we would die and leave her alone in the world, with no one to care for her. But if we fed ourselves, she would starve anyway . . . And my poor wife said to me, "I'd rather our daughter died a quick, painless death than this day by day starving." And we talked, and at last we agreed that I should take our little girl far from the city, and kill her quickly.'

'This story is one sin after another!' the monk said. 'Not fit for Christians to listen to!'

'So I walked away from the city hand in hand with my little girl,' said the rich man. 'I had a knife in my coat, ready to kill her. And she talked to me as we went, asking about the flowers and birds, until I couldn't keep from crying; and then she asked me why I cried. I couldn't do it, I couldn't kill her . . . I left her out there, in the wilds, and she was too small and too tired out to find her way home again. I hoped that she would die quickly of the cold in the night, or that wild animals would kill her – or that someone would find her and take care of her.'

'Terrible, cruel story,' said the monk, shaking his head.

'When I got home I couldn't tell my wife the truth,' said the rich man. 'I told her I had killed our little girl, and that she'd died in a moment, without any pain. But we were never happy after that. And when things began to be better for us – when I found work, and we began to have a little money and a little comfort – well, we felt even worse than before. My wife began to be so sad that she couldn't hold up her head, or stand on her feet for the weight of it. Our little girl was all she thought about, our little girl who we'd killed, and now we had the money to feed her fat and give her everything – but she was dead. And we never had any other children . . .'

'Did you ever tell her that you never killed the little girl?' the navvy asked.

'I did, but she thought I only said it to cheer her, and that it wasn't true. She took to her bed and couldn't lift her head from the pillow – and I, I worked, and made more and more money, and bought a fine house, and this carriage. But . . .'

'And have you tried to find out what happened to the little girl?' asked the navvy.

'Do you think I wouldn't have? I have sent men all over the country, asking questions, offering rewards – I would pay a fortune just to know for sure that she was dead. I've found out nothing.'

'It's a sad story all right,' says the navvy, 'but my ointment will cure your wife, you can be sure of that.'

'It had better,' says the rich man, 'because if it doesn't, after you've cured all those good-for-nothings, I shall have you arrested for a witch.'

'A witch!' says the navvy. 'I'm no witch!'

'No?' says the rich man. 'But you have a magic ointment that cures all ills. Only the Devil could have given you that. And if the Devil won't help you to cure my wife, I'll have you burned to ashes as a witch!'

'It is a difficult thing, to tell the difference between God working through a saint, and the Devil working through a witch,' said the monk. 'You see, the Devil can –'

'Ssh!' said First Born.

The carriage came to the rich man's house, and the rich man led the navvy up a big set of stairs and into the rich woman's room, where she lay with the curtains drawed to shut out the light, and the windows all tight shut to keep out the air. There she lay in the dark, in a big bed, not making a sound. A tray of food, all nicely set out, was on the table beside her. She hadn't et a thing.

'Sweetheart, my love, here's a doctor to cure you,' said her husband, and the navvy opened the little locket, dipped his finger in the ointment, rubbed it on the woman's forehead, and stood back, waiting for her to sit up and smile.

But she didn't move. She lay still in the bed, hid her face, and said not a thing.

'Wait a bit,' said the navvy. 'It might be taking a bit longer to work today.'

So they waited, but nothing happened. The navvy rubbed more ointment on the woman's head, but it did no good at all.

Then the rich man went to the door of the room, opened it and shouted, 'Come and arrest this witch!' And in came the King's officers – who he'd had waiting, ready – and they laid hold of the navvy, and he fought back, and in the struggle the locket, with the ointment, was dropped on the floor and kicked almost under the bed. Nobody noticed that because the navvy – I told you he was a strong lad – was putting up a hell of a fight; but in the end they got his arms, and they got his legs, and they carried him away to prison. And from prison he was brought to trial, and at the trial he was found guilty of being a tool of the Devil, and he was sentenced to be tied to a wooden post, and set alight, and burned into ashes.

And the day it was to be done come around, and there was the wooden post set up in the market-place, with all the wood for the burning stacked round it, and there sat the navvy in his prison-cell, trying to make the most of his last few, poor hours.

'He's going to be burned?' the monk asked. 'I can't think this is a good story, when such terrible things happen in it. Couldn't you have told us a better story – the childhood of a saint, maybe, that would have set a good example.'

'*For the love of God*!' cried a strange voice, a sharp-edged, commanding voice. 'Will you hold your unholy noise and let us hear the end in peace?'

The monk, and First Born, and Little Un all stared about them, and into the air, searching for the person who'd spoken.

'Such scant-witted, vulgar, untaught babblings as I've never had to tolerate,' went on the voice, and all their eyes turned to the same spot – to the open reliquary, and the little, shrivelled saint's head that grumbled in it. 'Go on, Droll, and if this jackass brays again, I promise you I'll stick his tongue to his teeth.'

Now the rich man's wife was still lying in her bed, in her dark room, not eating, not speaking, not moving. And by and by there comes a maid to tidy up, and the maid finds the locket on the floor, almost under the bed. And, thinking it belonged to her mistress, and that she'd dropped it, the maid picked it up and put it by the pillow.

And the rich woman, opening her eyes, saw the faint glimmer of the locket, and she opened her eyes wider. She sat up, she picked up the locket, she looked closely at it. And she opened her eyes and yelled for light.

In run a maid, carrying a lamp, and the rich woman looked at the locket in the light. Then up she got, and downstairs she ran, in her nightshirt. She went through room after room until she found her husband, and she shoved the locket under his nose.

But her husband was too glad to see his wife out of her bed and on her feet to care about the locket, and he tried to put his arms around her.

But she held him off. 'How did this come into the house?' she says. 'Where did this come from?'

Then he looked at it, and he says, 'Oh, that's the navvy's locket.'

'What navvy, what navvy?' she says.

'The navvy I brought here to cure you – but he was a cheat and a liar like all the rest.'

'Where is this navvy?' she says. 'Where is he?'

'Oh,' says the rich man. 'I had him arrested. He's to be burned in the market-place today.'

'Quickly!' yells the wife. 'We must speak with him!' And she rushes upstairs and dresses, and runs back down and sends for the carriage.

The rich man doesn't know what's going on, but he's so pleased to see his wife better that he'll go along with anything. So he drives with her to the prison, and he goes with her into the navvy's cell.

'Did you bring this into our house?' the woman asks, holding out the locket.

'Oh, the ointment did cure you then, after all,' says the navvy.

'No ointment cured me,' says the woman. 'This locket might. Did you bring it into our house?'

'Yes, it's mine,' says the navvy. 'I keep my ointment in it.'

'Where did you get it?' says the woman.

'It was give me by a goose-girl.'

'A goose-girl, a goose-girl!' cries the woman, and she says to her husband, 'You did tell the truth then, after all. You didn't kill our daughter – she's alive and she's a goose-girl! She had this locket around her neck on a ribbon when you

took her away, and now she's given it to him –
you must take us to her!' she says to the navvy.

And the navvy says, 'I'd be happy to try, but
I'm being burned today.'

So the woman turns to her husband and says,
'You must see to it that he isn't burned, but set
free, so he can take us to our daughter.'

Well, enough money can buy you anything, so
the rich man bribes the guards to go slow and
hold up the execution, and then he drives off to
the King's officers, and he pays more money,
and he argues, and says that the ointment did
cure his wife after all, so the navvy must be
working for God and not the Devil – and sure
enough, he gets everything changed. The navvy's set free, and he gets into the carriage with
the rich man and the rich woman, and he tells
them which way to go to find their daughter.

'Oh, isn't –?' the monk began, but Saint Unencumbere's head gave a cough, and he was quiet
at once.

Well, the navvy wasn't sure that he could find
the little house, because he'd looked for it once
before and couldn't find it. But he tries, and he
finds the right road first time – and instead of
crawling up to the door, half-dead, he drives up
in a carriage pulled by six black horses.

The hideous old hag was sitting on the bench
outside her door, shelling peas into a basin, and
she knowed the navvy when he stepped down
from the carriage. 'What, have you made your
fortune?' she shouts out.

'I've come looking for your daughter,' he says.

94

The rich man and woman got down behind him, and they got a bit of a shock when they saw what the hag looked like, but then the woman says,

'I'm looking for my daughter, who used to wear this locket. Is she with you? Please let me see her.'

'*Your* daughter,' says the old hag. 'She's been my daughter since I found her wandering and took her in.'

Then the woman and the man begun to cry, and the woman said, 'Oh, please let me see her, even if she never knows I'm her mother, even if you keep her with you, let me see her and know that she's safe and happy.'

The old hag leans into the house and shouts, 'Little Puddin', me petal, me rose, come out here.'

And out come the young hag, uglier than a box of grubs, big-nosed, small-eyed, thin as a knife and stinking like a cesspit. That quietened the rich man and woman. They stood staring.

But then the rich woman says, 'Oh, my poor little girl, what hard living's done to you! How starved you are! Come home with us now and I'll give you everything I wasn't able to give you –' And then the woman went and hugged the ugly goose-girl, hugged her tight and cried over her and said, 'I've found my little girl.'

The old hag had been watching all this, and now she says, 'Why don't you go and wash, daughter, ready for your journey?'

And the rich woman says, 'I'll come with you – I'll wash your back and rinse your hair.'

So down went the young hag, the goose-girl, and the rich woman to the pool under the apple tree. And, this time, the navvy was careful to keep his back turned to the pool and his eyes on the house. But all happened just as he'd seen it before: the young hag took off all her clothes, and then her skin, and stepped into the pool as a lovely young girl. The rich woman kept her mouth shut for wonder, and washed the girl's back, and rinsed through her long dark hair; and then helped her dry herself. 'Don't put those clothes back on,' she said. 'I have better for you in the carriage.' And when she was dressed in her new clothes and came back to the house arm in arm with her new mother, the girl looked so beautiful that the young navvy felt very sad, because she was a rich girl now and would never look at him.

'What do you say, daughter?' asks the old hag. 'Are you happy to go with your mother and father now they've found you?'

'If they'd turned up their noses at me when they saw me as the goose-girl, I would have stayed with you,' said the girl. 'But since they still wanted me, I'll go with them.'

'And you,' says the rich man to the old hag, 'you must come with us and be taken care of too – you took care of our little girl for so many years. Come with us, and I'll see that you have all you wish for the rest of your life.'

'For the rest of *my* life?' said the old hag. 'That would be a longer time than you could guess. And don't you see my geese here? Every one of them is a poor lost soul, and I must take care of them – no one else will.' And, since they couldn't understand what she meant, and couldn't persuade her to take a step away from her house, they all got back into the carriage and drove away.

When they got back to the city, the navvy thought he'd have to say goodbye and be on his way, but the rich man asked him to stay with them a while – 'Because I treated you badly,' said the rich man, 'and I want to make it up to you.' So the navvy stayed with them, and he grew fonder and fonder of their beautiful daughter, who had pulled him out of the thorn bushes and healed his cuts and his blindness with her ointment. And the lovely girl – who now wore the locket round her neck again – grew fonder and fonder of him, because he was a fine, strong, pretty lad after all, and she didn't need to marry for money. And the end of it was, the navvy and the lovely girl got married, and if they didn't live happily ever after, at least they had a grand time while it lasted.

And she give the locket to her daughter, and she give it to her daughter, and she give it to hers, and it's still around – but the ointment lost its goodness long ago, and that's why there's still so much pain and sickness in the world, mercy on us.

The children rolled on their backs, lay flat on the grass and sighed. The monk took a deep, deep breath, bowed his head, and he sighed too. There was quiet for a time. The river rolled by. The breeze shook the leaves and broke the light into spangles. In the water, the moorhens cruised and the ducks splashed. The heat of the sun poured down, and soaked into the earth and into their skins.

'Well, are you rested, me babbies?' Linnet asked. 'We've got to get on.'

'Where to?' asked the girl, lying on her back with her eyes closed.

'Go on along this river until you come on a stream running into it – you'll know the stream, there's a church on the hill above it. Are you listening?'

'A church on the hill above it,' said the girl, to show she was.

'Climb up the hill, following the stream – oh, and you'll come to The Cat and Fiddle by and by – I'll tell you as you go.'

'A cat with a fiddle?' said First Born, and opened her eyes. She rolled on her side, and then said, 'Look at the saint!'

They looked and saw that, though the saint's head was still brown and wrinkled, it was no longer withered. The brown was now the brown of tanned skin, and there seemed to be a flush of blood in the cheeks. The eyes had opened, and they were brown and bright. Seeing them all looking at her, the saint smiled, and showed big yellow teeth, with a few black gaps. 'Thank you for the story, Droll, and God bless you,' she said. 'How many, many years since I heard a good tale like that.'

The monk looked off into the trees and said, 'A very unchristian tale, *I* thought it.'

'Oh, be quiet you ignoramus! A good enough lad, he means well,' said the saint to Linnet's head, 'but he is a trial to me. What do you know of good tales or bad tales or unchristian tales?' the saint shouted, though she couldn't turn in her reliquary to see the monk. 'How long have

98

you lived? How many have you heard? How many of the heathen have you converted? Who are you to say what's unchristian? Are you a saint, you long gobdaw?'

The monk hung his head and said nothing.

The saint's head sat in its little box, smiling to itself, and when no one spoke, it thought they were afraid of it and smiled more. It shouted, 'Come here, you lummox!'

The monk knelt beside the reliquary.

'Get off your knees, what use are you to me on your knees? I want you to take me back to my own chapel – at once!'

'But I can't –' the monk began.

'Don't tell me, "can't"! Who are you going to obey – some belly-stuffed, bone-brained Abbot or one of God's Holy Saints? I won't go to France at my age. I never wanted to go there when I was alive, and I'll go to Hell first now. Well, gowk, moon-fisher, rattle-head, what are you going to do?'

The monk hung his head, twisted his hands together, and at last said, 'I'm going to take you home, Your Holiness.'

'Of course you are. And put the story-teller in a bag and bring him with us. I shall need him to tell me a story every day.'

'Oh no,' Linnet said. 'A pleasure to tell you one story, love, but I'm taking me babbies home.'

'Your pups don't matter; God's work does – and I need your –'

But First Born had scooped up her father's head, grubby old shirt and all, and was running away through the grass and trees with her brother after her.

'Catch them!' yelled Saint Unencumbere. 'Up, lump, and after them!'

But the monk shook his head. 'I'll carry you back, Madam, to the monastery, even though I shall be in trouble – and I'll ask that you be told a story every day, if you'd like that – but let the children go.'

The saint's head tut-tutted and grumbled, but then closed its eyes. 'Oh very well. But no long-winded maunderings about the saints,' it added, as the monk began to close the reliquary. 'Spare me the Little Flowers for the love of God . . . And don't catch my beard in the hinges!'

5

A smiling tabby cat was playing on a fiddle and
dancing a jig. Behind it, in an indigo sky filled
with gold stars, a red dappled cow jumped over
a white crescent moon. That was the picture
painted on the wooden sign swinging at the top
of the pole outside the inn: The Cat and Fiddle.

It was an inn for travellers on a road that
crossed the high moors. Up its walls rose from
the dark green, tussocky grass, the only walls for
miles. It held its black roof against the grey sky,
and the wind whined through its chimneys, or
blew down them hollowly, with a sound like that
of a giant boy blowing across the mouth of a
bottle. Grey stone were the inn walls, and black
slate its roof. The only colour about it was the
rowan tree that grew close to one corner.

Bright green, bright red, the rowan, the very
colours of life and magic. Green for growth, and
the berries the same clear fresh red as the blood
that comes from a cut finger. As the wind blew,
the rowan laid its pretty pointed green leaves
against the grey wall, struck the brilliant red of
its berries against the grey stone.

The inn yard was not well kept. The hollows
between the cobbles held mud and horse-dung,
and thriving tufts of the moorland grass which
was forever creeping in to cover the yard again.

On the other side of the inn's door was a draughty hall, where bare grey floorboards had been scuffed and marked by muddy, nailed boots. A gaunt and dusty flight of stairs climbed up into darkness. But, from behind the door beside the stairs came the sounds of voices and glasses. In that room, a fire burned, and gathered around it, in comfortable chairs and comfortable chat, were a magistrate and a doctor, a schoolmaster and a clergyman. They had a drink each, and, on a table near them, was a plate piled high with meaty sandwiches.

The door of their snug opened, and they all turned their heads, and were all surprised and amused to see two beggar children come in. The older was a girl of twelve or so, dressed in a woman's old dress which hung emptily, in clumsy bags and folds about her skinny body. Its fraying hem had been cut short about her ankles. Over the dress she wore what seemed to be a man's old shirt with no collar; and a shapeless man's hat was crammed on to her head. Her hair was tucked up into it, to keep it from the rain. Her feet stuck out at the bottom of the frayed hem: bony, bare, and red and purple with cold and wet.

'A little breath of fashion *Parisienne* has blown unto us, gentlemen,' said the magistrate, and his friends all laughed quietly, cocking their heads to look at each other and share the joke.

The other child was a boy, who held his sister's hand. His trousers had once belonged to a full-grown man. The legs had been cut short, but the seat bagged low. His shirt, which he wore like a coat, hanging almost to his feet, was a man's shirt. He had no hat, and his hair was wet.

'Perhaps the young man will buy us all a drink,' said the doctor, and sent another laugh rippling round among his friends. To the children he spoke more sharply. 'What are you doing? You shouldn't be in here.'

The boy looked up at his sister. The girl said nothing, but led her brother to the corner under the window, at a distance from the men, and made him sit down against the wall. She sat beside him, and began to unwrap a bundle she carried. She set it on her lap, and undid knots, and unfolded cloth from around it.

The magistrate huffed to himself, and said to the doctor, 'Your authority, my friend, sets them all of a tremble. What is it she has there? Is it their dinner?'

'Someone else's dinner, perhaps,' said the doctor. 'They really should not be in here. They'll smell worse than wet dogs soon.'

'My God!' said the schoolmaster, so suddenly, and sounding so unlike his usual self, that all his friends turned towards him, to find him staring, in alarm, at the children. All at the same moment, they turned to look at the children, and saw what it was that the girl had unwrapped.

In her lap lay a man's head, cut through the neck. It was a horrible shock to see it lying there. The clergyman's hand tightened hard around his glass, and sloshed port on to his clerical bands, while the magistrate's arm leaped and threw his glass away. It smashed on the floor. The little boy looked up at the sound, but the girl didn't. She was busy.

She had lifted up a corner of the cloth the head

had been wrapped in and moistened it at her mouth. Gently, she used the cloth to wipe the face of the head in her lap, like a mother cleaning a child. And when she had washed the face, she began to comb out the long hair with her fingers.

The men at the fire looked at each other, amazed, wondering, and saw how the faces of the others had paled. 'They should not be in here,' said the doctor. 'Monsters, little monsters.'

The schoolmaster made a choking noise, and once more they all looked at him. He was half-raised from his chair, gaping at the children. Already feeling dread, they looked where he looked.

The head still lay in the girl's lap, and its eyes had opened, in an angry stare. As they watched – they could not look away – the lips parted in the beard, and the tip of a tongue came out. It licked along the upper lips, and then the lips were pursed together. 'Good day, gentlemen,' said the head, in a dry, sore-throated voice – and surely the throat of a severed head must be always sore?

The doctor, the magistrate, the schoolmaster and the clergyman sat pressed against their chair-backs, stock-still and appalled.

The girl got to her knees, holding the head carefully between her hands. Getting to her feet, she came forward and set the head on the table beside the sandwiches, before scurrying back across the floor and whisking into her corner.

The head lolled on the table among the rags that had wrapped it, and it froze them cold to see it lying there, with every appearance of life. The skin was tanned and weathered to a tawny brown that glowed as if blood still ran beneath it. The eyes, that looked quickly from one to another of them, were bright and clear: brown eyes, speckled with green and gold lights and edged with black lashes. And all around the head was the thick growth of dark hair, hanging over the brow and trailing on the table in coiling dark strands – though the beard was striped silver-grey at each corner of the mouth. The schoolmaster, when the quick eyes moved to him, covered his face with a hand and turned away.

The corners of the head's mouth moved easily back, baring strong teeth in a smile that was not friendly. 'I mean you no harm, gentlemen,' it said. 'I come to do you what service I can . . . I've no feet and no hands to dig with anymore, but I've a head full of stories and a tongue between my teeth – so how about a story, gentlemen, to pass the time?'

There was no answer from the gentlemen who, pinned to their chairs with horror, could find neither words to say nor breath to speak them. Slowly they turned their eyes to look at each other, and seeing the others' faces all blanched, turned their eyes back to the head.

'A story then,' said the head, 'and though me babbies are dressed unfashionable and smell worse than dogs, you'll tolerate 'em in the corner there until I'm done. And the story shall be – *A Dream of Hell*.'

Come you all, come and harken, harken to the tale of a master and his servant on a day as cold as frozen Hell.

Aye, on a day so cold it froze your tongue to your teeth, when the birds froze in the air and shattered when they hit the ground, a day that squeezed the blood out of your hands and feet – on this cold day, out drives the master to collect his rents. He goes in a coach, o'course, in his fur-lined coat and his fur-lined hat and gloves, with blankets over his knees and brandy to warm him. And up in front, driving, is his coachman, John, with the wind spearing him to his seat and flaying his face.

They're driving along, with John's hands freezing to the reins, and his eyes closed by the wind, when the master bangs with his stick and yells, 'Pull up, pull up!'

John pulls up, and there's a house by the roadside and a family being turned out. There's their table standing on the white grass at the side of the road, and there's their chairs stacked on top. There's all the family, wrapped in all the clothes they own, and hugging themselves, and the children trying to get out of the wind by standing behind their dad – but the wind's blowing straight through his ribs, so that's no good. And there – pulled up at the side of the road – is another coach, and whose coach is it? The parson's, that's who.

'Good day, Parson, good day,' calls out John's master. 'An eviction, eh?'

The parson raises his flask to John's master and says, 'Couldn't pay their tithe, y'know, so out they go.'

'Very good, give God his due!' says John's master, and bangs with his stick again. 'On, John, on!'

So John whips up the horses and on they go. Here and there they stop, and the master leans out the coach window and watches his rent collected. Even if it takes the last penny out a man's pocket, the master leans there and smiles as he watches it go into his rent-collector's leather satchel. And when a woman says she can't pay, the master bawls, 'Get the money by Friday next or out you go, out you go!'

She comes running down the path, shivering in her dress and shawl to stand by the coach window and say, 'But we've paid the tithe to the church, and we've paid the poll-taxes, and now we can't find the rent as well!'

The master draws in his head and rolls up the window. 'You have your house and I must have my rent,' he says. 'I give you till Friday next, that's generous. Find it, or out you go. On John, on!'

And on they go, with the wind blowing a blast past John's ears and scraping the hair off his face. His finger-nails and his toe-nails feel like nails all right – like iron nails, nailing his fingers to his palms and his toes to his boots. And they come to a roadside inn – just like this one, gentlemen, just like this one – and the yard outside's full of coaches and horses.

'Pull up, pull up!' shouts the master. 'This is where I dine!'

So John pulls into the yard, and out gets his master, who thinks it's a bit nippy in the yard, so he skips into the inn pretty fast. 'See to the horses, John,' he says, 'and you can step inside for a while.'

It takes John a while longer to get down from

the box than it took his master to run inside. It takes him five minutes to let go off the reins, and then his hands stay frozen in the grip. His knees have froze, his shoulders have froze; his back's froze into a hump. Down he comes, slow, slow, scared to jump in case he breaks.

He has to unshackle the horses, but he can't move his fingers, he's so cold, so cold. And he has to walk the horses up and down, and see that they're stabled afore he can limp across the yard – his toes are so cold, they hurt at every step – and go inside the inn himself.

Inside the inn there's a big room and a big fire, and sitting next to the fire is John's master. And next to him there's the parson, and next to him the magistrate, and next to him another master, and another and another – all of 'em gathered round the fire like so many fire-screens, not letting a bit of heat get past 'em and into the rest of the room. And John's master sees him come in and points and says, 'There's food and drink set out for you there, John.'

And John looks and there, in a corner, away from the fire, in the draught from under the door, there's a bench, and a table with a pint pot and a pie on it. So John goes and sits in the corner, and he pulls his coat round him, tucks his hand under his oxters, stamps his feet and gets as warm as he can. Not a breath of heat from the fire can he feel.

But John puts his head back against the hard wall behind him, and he dozes off – and he dozes, and dozes – until he wakes with a yell and falls off his bench and kicks the table over – and all the gentry jump and look round from the fire: 'What? What?'

'John, my man, whatever's the matter?' says his master. 'What's all the noise about?'

'Sorry, sir, sorry,' says John. 'Only I fell asleep, sir, and I had a dream.'

'A bad dream, I think, from the clatter,' says his master.

'Oh a bad dream, aye,' says John. 'I dreamt of Hell.'

'A dream of Hell?' says the parson, and smirks round at all the masters. 'Do tell us, John – what was Hell like?'

'The truth, sir,' says John. 'Hell was just like this inn.'

And all the masters laughed. 'Well, Parson, *you've* never told us that!' said John's master. 'Hell – just like this inn! I think I might like Hell! How was Hell like an inn, John?'

And John says, 'I couldn't get near the fires for rich folk and clergy.'

The head laughed its sore-throated laugh, and said, 'Oh, the fires of Hell burn high with rich folk and clergy – ask Parson – he'll preach it to you next Sunday.'

The parson, the schoolmaster, the magistrate and the doctor sat silent while the story sank into their minds, and then they rose and pushed back their chairs, and beckoned the two children to come forward to the fire. The children came slowly, but more quickly once they could see the head smiling at them. They crouched on the hearth, rubbing the heat of the flames into their arms and squeezing the water out of their clothes and hair. The doctor handed them down the plate of sandwiches; and the gentlemen all withdrew their chairs to a distance and watched as the children chewed their own fingers in their haste to eat. The schoolmaster went out to find the landlord, and brought the children back cake and milk.

The head lay on the table, the lids and lashes lowered over its eyes as it watched the children, and its mouth sad. When there was only one sandwich left, the girl reached up and lifted down the head and all its wrappings. She tucked it in the crook of her arm, and its long dark hair coiled over her sleeve and shoulder. Lifting her cup of milk, she set it to the head's lips, while the little boy tore off a lump of bread and, when the cup was taken from the head's lips, he put the bread into its mouth.

Then the girl set the head and its wrappings on the hearth-rug, and she once more tried to tidy its hair with her fingers. As she stroked and combed, the head began to speak in a low voice, softer than the one it had used to tell the story, and meant only for the children.

'Keep on this road,' it said. 'Don't turn off it anywhere, and it'll bring you to a town, a big, dirty town. That's the place you want.'

The girl nodded as she went on combing, and the head's eyes closed heavily, opened slowly, closed again. Then the eyes stayed shut while the lips, edged with dark and grey beard, were a little open. The head seemed in a deep sleep.

The girl lifted the edges of the cloth that the head rested in, and folded the cloth and knotted it until the head could no longer be seen. Then she stood, and lifted the bundle by a fold of cloth. Taking her brother by the hand, she helped him to his feet and, with a shy smile at the gentlemen, led him from the room and out of the inn.

The gentlemen sat on in the room, their chairs dragged back from the fire. They sat without a word to each other. Then the schoolmaster rose and, with a muttered goodbye, left; and the doctor went soon after him. The magistrate and the clergyman sat on a while longer, but then rose almost together and went home.

And none of them ever spoke of the children and the head, because each had determined, in his own mind, that it had been a dream and not worth mentioning.

6

The bricks of the pub wall were outlined with strips of moss, and streaked with green. Miners sat on the steps, their clothes sagging with wear, their faces blackened. Their mouths, washed clean by beer, were comically red, their eyes and teeth gleaming white, against the coal-dust. To them came two grimy, bedraggled children, the older girl leading the little boy by the hand and carrying, in the crook of her other arm, a filthy bundle of rags.

The girl stopped in front of the pub step, and said to the men sitting on it, 'Game for a bet, lads?'

The men looked at her, and they looked at each other, and they laughed.

'What have you got to bet, my lover?'

The girl looked at her brother, who felt carefully in the shreds of one pocket, and produced a farthing, which he held out on one hand. The miners leaned forward to look, and then sat back and laughed again.

'A farthing,' said the girl. 'Nothing to them with money – but a fortune to them without. We're betting all we have, lads – are you game?'

'Aye,' said the man who sat in the middle of the step. 'I'm game.' And he took from his pocket a penny, and held it up to more laughter from his friends. 'A whole penny, cocker. What's the bet?'

The girl let go of her brother's hand and held out the bundle of muddied, torn and dirty rags. 'I bet you can't guess what's in my bundle without untying it.'

'You're on,' said the man, and put his penny down on a brick stepping-stone that stuck up from the mud of the street.

'And me,' said the man beside him, and placed a second penny beside the first.

The girl came forward with her bundle, put her farthing down beside the pennies, and handed the bundle over to the miner. More and more blackened hands reached out, and more and more pennies were placed on the brick, as the first miner began to feel and squeeze the ragged, dirty bundle between his hands.

'Clothes,' he said.

The girl shook her head.

The man felt the bundle again. 'Something round. Something hard. A football, is it?'

The girl shook her head.

'Give it here,' said another miner. He took the bundle and felt it with hard squeezes. 'A turnip,' he said. 'A swede.'

'You can't have two guesses,' his mate said. 'Which is it?'

'A swede.'

Another man came out of the pub, and was greeted with laughs and shouts of, 'Here he is! What you going to put down, Such?'

Such was better dressed than the miners, in a dark suit with a bright, shimmering waistcoat. He was clean; he owned the pub. 'A half-crown,' he said, and put the silver coin on the brick with the copper. He took the bundle, and felt it, and said, squinting one of his eyes as he spoke, 'It's a big stone wrapped up in clothes, to trick us.'

All the men came crowding forward, putting down pennies and half-pennies and reaching out for their turn to feel the bundle. It was a swede, they said, or a stone, or a football, or a round bowl.

'Now let's see what it is, my love,' said Such, and handed the bundle back to the girl.

She knelt down on the muddy ground and untied and unwrapped the bundle – and the miners drew back, and stared, and swallowed at the sight of the head, without neck or shoulders, or any body at all, lying aslant on its own thick, dark hair. Slowly they raised their eyes from the head to the girl and the boy.

'I win,' said the girl, and she nodded to the boy who gathered all the coins into his pockets. 'Another bet?' asked the girl.

'What?' asked Such, eyeing the head sidelong. 'Are you going to bet us it can talk?'

'Aye,' said the girl.

There was a murmuring amongst the miners, and they rose and stepped back from the head, and the boy and girl, before crouching again, to see and listen.

Such reached out and touched the cheek of the head, and hurriedly withdrew his hand quickly from the cold flesh, holding it away from him as if it was smeared with something he didn't want to get on his clothes. 'If you can make that head speak,' he said, 'I'll give you a crown.'

As soon as he finished speaking, before the

girl's smile had spread across her mouth, the blue lids of the head were seen to roll upwards to show bright brown eyes. White teeth showed through its beard, between its lips. 'Nobody makes me speak,' it said. 'I choose when to speak. Good day to you, Such.'

Such stooped and looked more closely at the head's face, squinting again. 'Jesus God,' he said. 'I know you . . . Do I know you?'

'I knew you, before I left to dig the canals. Now I'm on me way back again, and I can't turn up on me mother's door, with two babbies and no money – so pay up that crown, Such.'

Such sank down into a crouch, staring into the head's face. From his pocket he took a crown.

'Another bet?' asked the head. 'You always liked a bet, Such. Another bet, lads? Can you answer me a riddle in three guesses?'

Many of the miners drew still further off, though they still hung on the edges of the crowd, listening. Such put down a golden guinea. Miners leaned forward, adding coppers, and silver threepennies, even sixpences, to the pile of coins on and around the brick, betting on Such or against him. 'Give us your riddle,' Such said.

The head smiled, its stiff, dark-bearded lips drawing back over white teeth. It said: *'Riddle Me This?'*

A man had a bull, a white bull, a bull whose hide shone like sugar or the full moon or ox-eye daisies in a meadow. And this bull was big, so big that if you started at its tail and rode on a fast horse, rode all day at a gallop, from dawn till noon, you'd have reached its middle, about where the sirloins stop and the best rib cuts begin. Then, if you changed horses, and rode at a gallop from noon till dark, you'd reach the bull's nose, shining white in the dusk. So this was a bloody big bull. It'd fetch a good price. So its master took it to market to sell it.

But he hadn't gone far on the road before an eagle, a rushing golden eagle, flared out of the sky, sank its talons in the bull, and carried it off and away, over forests, over rivers, over the hills and high and far away.

The eagle was hungry, so it was looking for somewhere to land and get its beak into those sirloins and rib chops. Looking down with its golden eyes, it saw a shepherd in a valley, with his flock: white woolly sheep against green grass. There was a ram in the flock with fine curly horns. Down flew the eagle and landed on a curl of the ram's horns. It held the bull under one claw and tore into it.

Now it come on to rain, and the shepherd brought himself and his whole flock to shelter under the ram's belly. And there they all were, peering out at the rain through the hanging wool, when the shoulder-blade of the bull – torn loose by the eagle – come wheeling down through the air and went straight into the shepherd's eye.

The shepherd blinked and blinked – he pulled his upper lid down over his lower lid – he rubbed his eye – but he couldn't get rid of what was bothering him. And it bothered him so much that he took his flock home early, through the rain, led them back down to the village and penned them up. And he started to complain, 'I've

116

got something in me eye! There's something in me eye, and it's sore.'

All his neighbours come to look, but none of them could get rid of whatever it was in his eye. So they sent for a doctor, but he was no good, and he sent for another doctor. And the second doctor sent for a third, and the third sent for a fourth, until there were six doctors – and the sixth doctor brought a rowing boat and a fishing net with him because the others had told him to. The six doctors pushed the rowing boat off into the shepherd's eye, and climbed aboard, and all six of them rowed out into the middle of the shepherd's eye, dipping their oars in his eye-water. They cast the net overboard, and they rowed round and round the shepherd's eye, until they dredged up the bull's shoulder-blade. 'Ah! That's what's been causing the trouble!' they said.

They showed the shepherd the bone, and they said, 'No need to pay us. We've enjoyed the day's fishing.'

'Bloody eagle,' said the shepherd, and throwed the shoulder-blade high in the air, so it sailed over the houses of the village and landed with a crash a mile away.

There it lay, shining in the moonlight and, when a gang of navvies came by on the tramp, tramp, tramp, they thought it was a lake shining in the moonlight, and they camped by it for the night. But as they slept, there began a crunching, grating, growling that woke them in a fright. It was a fox that had got its teeth around the blade-bone and was crunching and cracking it. So the navvies grabbed their catapults, and stones, and they killed the fox. Then they skinned it – but the fox was so big that they couldn't turn it over, and they took the skin off only one side of it.

There was a woman with the navvies who had a newborn baby, and they gave her the fox-skin to make clothes for it. But, 'It's too small,' she says. 'Where's the rest of it?'

'Still on the fox,' says the navvies. 'Biggest fox you ever saw. If you can get the rest of it, you're welcome to it.'

So the woman went to where the fox was lying, carrying her baby in one arm, and when she came to the fox, she turned it over with one hand. She took off the rest of the fox-skin and, when she added it to the other half, it was just big enough, and not a hair bigger – to make her baby a fox-fur cap.

So here's the question, here's the asking – riddle me, riddle me, riddle me this – which was the biggest, which the greatest, the tallest, the bulkiest, the hulkingest – which cast the longer shadow, which trod the deeper footprint?

Was it the bull so long that it took a whole day to ride past it? Was it the eagle that carried such a long bull off and ate it? Or the sheep? How about the shepherd who was so big, the bull's shoulder blade sank in his eye? The doctors? The navvies who camped by the shoulder-blade or the fox who came and chewed it? The woman who skinned the fox, or the newborn baby who wore a cap of its fur?

Riddle me the biggest, the biggest of all these. Not the smallest, nor the middling, but the biggest, without doubt, without question, the biggest – one answer each. The biggest, lads, the biggest.

The circle of listening men continued silent. Their heads turned and they looked at each other. They shook their heads and pulled long mouths. More and more faces turned to Such.

'The bull?' said Such at last, and was immediately shoved and punched by those around him.

'The eagle carried off the bull, noggin-head!'

'Bull was smallest!'

'Bull!'

'I'm a fool,' Such said, and leaned his chin in his hand, and scowled as he thought. Then he raised one finger and said slowly, 'It was – the baby.'

'No,' said the head.

'But the fox-fur – the baby's cap – '

'The baby was bigger than the fox, and the fox gnawed the bull's bone – but the baby wasn't the biggest thing in the story. One more guess.'

'Come on, Such!'

'Think!'

'You can get it – think now!'

'Well,' Such said, 'if it isn't the baby . . . then . . . it must be . . . the mother!'

'No,' said the head, and there was a great outcry of groans and laughter. The boy and the girl gathered up all the coins, copper, silver, gold, and poured them into pockets, tied them in rags.

'All right, all right, you win,' Such said. 'What is the answer? Which was the biggest?'

The head asked, 'Is me mother still living in the same old place, Such?'

'As far as I know.'

'Put me babbies on the right road, then, and I'll tell you the answer.'

'Easy,' Such said. 'Follow this road out of town, keep on it for a mile, you'll come to a little stream runs over the road. Just past that's some pigsties and a row of three cottages. Your Granny lives in the middle one. Now – the answer.'

And Such bent down and First Born lifted the head up, and the head whispered the answer in Such's ear. No one else heard, and Such didn't tell.

The girl, her skirt sagging with the weight of money tied into it, swiftly wrapped and folded the head's dark hair from sight, tied it all up like a pudding cloth or a workman's dinner, took her little brother by the hand and walked away.

Behind them, the miners watched them go and, when they were out of sight, all began to argue. They left the muddy street and went inside the pub, where they could crouch against the bar and sit on benches and argue. The answer was in the story. Which was the biggest? Tell it over and over, the answer is in the story – which was the biggest?

7

Frost was whitening the stones of the road, flattening and whitening the grasses that grew beside it. In the trees, among green and golden leaves, hung bunches of berries, fiercely red. The cold wind touched more leaves, withering them to gold, and brought a whiff of coming Christmas. Those who could manage their business indoors were glad to do so, and kept close to whatever little bit of fire they could afford.

A woman heard a knock at her door, opened it a crack, to let in as little cold air as she could, and saw two small figures standing out there, darker lumps in the darkness. She waited for them to speak.

First Born and Little Un, having come so far and reached home at last, had nothing to say, and stood waiting to be let into the warm.

'What?' said the woman, when they didn't speak. Getting no answer, she pulled the door wider, dragging it over the rough earth floor, and letting the dim red light of the fire fall on her visitors. She saw two children, their hair long, dirty and matted; their clothes damp, dirty, crumpled; their feet wrapped in rags. Poor cold little things, she thought, thieves though they certainly were. 'And what do you want?'

Still they didn't answer, but simply stood, side

by side outside her door, looking up at her. Her eyes grew used to the outer dark, and she saw their faces more clearly: thin, pale little faces, stained by wind-tears, with chapped lips and red, running noses. 'Oh – come in for a bit,' the woman said, reluctant to stand in the cold herself any longer, but unable to close the door on those cold children.

They came into the single room of the house, and she shoved the door closed before turning to look at them, feeling foolish for having been so weak as to let them in. More than likely, they would steal everything she had. And what when their parents came looking for them, if they bothered? Wretched little tinker brats. She should have been sensible and shut the door on them. After all, if they were cold and hungry, it wasn't her fault, nor her job to look after them.

The smaller child was standing in the middle of the little room, hugging itself and staring at her. The older had crouched down and was unwrapping a filthy bundle. 'I'm not buying anything, so you needn't bother,' said the woman, thinking the child was about to show her some gypsy trash it had for sale.

The child folded back the last layer of cloth and looked up at her. The woman looked down on two firelit faces – the child's and, below that, another face, where no face could or should be. It lay on the floor, among the folds of an old shirt and the coils of its own hair. She calmly stared at it for what seemed a long time, recognizing the face and knowing that she did, but unable to remember where she had seen it. 'It's a head only,' she thought to herself. 'There is no body, only a head.' And yet the head was not horrible.

It had her son's face: her son who had gone to earn good money digging the canals. Her son's head, cut from his body, brought to her by two tinker brats.

The shock shook her to her knees, and brought her closer to the head. She knelt there, her hands to her mouth.

The eyes of the head slowly opened, and her son looked at her. She forgot to be afraid, forgot that there was nothing but a head lying there, so living and natural was the look he gave her. His lips parted in his grey and brown beard, and he smiled. 'All the money I made, I spent – but I've brought money and – me babbies.'

Her head whipped round, and she stared at the children.

'They'll be better with you,' said the head, 'than among the navvies.'

The woman, still kneeling, went on staring at the children, stared and stared at them. She peered through the shifting firelight, through the marks of cold and weariness, through the dirt, searching for a likeness to her son. The children looked back at her, hoping to find kindness in her face.

'I've two favours to ask you,' said the head. 'The first one is, look after me babbies.'

'As if I wouldn't take care of me own grand-children!' said the woman angrily. 'As if you have to ask!'

'But if I hadn't asked, you wouldn't have liked it,' said the head. 'I've one favour to ask, then. Wrap me again, and bury me.'

The girl, still kneeling by the head, said, 'No!'

'Bury me,' said the head. 'Bury me under the

123

hearthstone, under the talk and the eating, and I'll keep luck in the house. Bury me under the doorstep, under the coming and going, and I'll let nothing harmful in. Or bury me under the apple tree in the yard, and I'll grow the sweetest apples in seven counties. But bury me.'

'No!' said the woman.

'Stay and tell us stories,' said Little Un.

'Without you, we won't know what to do,' said First Born.

'Who is their mother?' asked the woman. 'Or who was she? Where have you been – how did you die?'

'Bury me. Hearthstone, doorstep or apple tree, but bury me.'

'Stay with us – I'll wash your shirt and wrap you in it clean.'

'You shall have a dish to lie in,' said the woman, 'or a box! A box, lined, on the hearth, and you'll see everything and hear everything, and tell us stories every day.'

The head's eyes closed, and a sigh came from its mouth. 'Put me on the hearth, then,' it said, 'and I'll tell you a story.'

So the head, pillowed on the folds of the dirty old shirt, was put on the floor by the hearth, in the full light of the fire; and the woman drew the two children closer to the warmth and sat them down while she found them some food. Even while she looked into her cupboard, she kept her face turned towards the head. The children, finding nothing wonderful in their father's head, watched her.

'I shall tell,' said the head, 'of – *King Arthur's Christmas.*'

When good King Arthur ruled this land,
He was a thievin' king.
He stole three sacks of barley meal
To make a bag-puddin'.
A bag-puddin' the King did make
And stuffed it well with plums;
He put in it great lumps of fat
As big as both me thumbs.
And all the knights and horses did of that puddin'
    dine,
And what they couldn't eat that night, the Queen
    next mornin' fried.

Oh, you'll have heard tell of Arthur, the thieving plum-puddin' lover, Arthur ap Uther, Pendragon, High King over all the kings of the Isles of Britain. Arthur, who had a cloak trimmed with the beards of all the kings and emperors he'd defeated, a hairy cloak, black, yellow, white, red, brown, grizzled.

But have you heard tell how Arthur, on Christmas Day, wouldn't eat or drink until news of some wonder, some strangeness in his land, had been brought to him? No, he wouldn't eat a crust nor even a bit of plum-puddin', he wouldn't drink a drop of water, he wouldn't even seat hisself at his round table, until he'd heard tell of some miracle.

And it happened one Christmas, while Arthur was walking round and round Camelot, with his throat dry and his belly rumbling, that Gawaine came running to find him, and he said, 'Come to the feast-hall, Uncle, come and take your place, quickly! Merlin has brought your wonder!'

So Arthur went back to the feast-hall, and

there was Merlin – you'll have heard of him, Merlin the witch, the spell-maker, the wise man. And with Merlin was a man dressed in golden armour.

Now Arthur took a good look at this man, because *he* hadn't got any golden armour, for all he was High King of Britain. The man was the tallest man in Camelot, a small giant. His golden breastplate was shaped like the muscles of a bared body, but there was a blazing sun at its centre. He wore a linen skirt and, on his legs, golden greaves. His forearms were covered with golden guards, and under one arm he carried a golden helmet with two white plumes, one on either side. But the man inside this shining armour was old. His head was stooped forward, and his face lined and sagging. The muscles of his arms were growing loose.

'You are welcome, Sir Knight,' said Arthur, thinking that this armoured man was surely a knight, if a strange one. 'Set him a chair!' But, as Gawaine brought a chair for their guest, Arthur said quietly to Merlin, 'Is this my wonder? An old man?'

'Ask his name,' said Merlin.

And so Arthur asked his guest for his name, but the old man shook his head and did not understand, until Merlin spoke a charm. Then the old man said, 'I am Alexander.'

'And I am Arthur,' said Arthur. 'But who is Alexander? Whose son is Alexander? What is Alexander's country?'

The old man raised his head again and said, 'I am Alexander, the son of Philip. My country is Macedon, but my kingdom stretches from

Greece to India. What is *your* country?'

Merlin spoke to the old man then, and he said, 'This King before you is that Arthur who drew the sword from the stone. Do you dare to face him and claim to be that Alexander who conquered Persia?'

The old man said, 'I am Alexander.'

'Who led his armies to the end of the world? Who was made a god in Egypt?'

'I am Alexander.'

'Who rode the horse Bukephalos? Who was undefeated in battle?'

'I am Alexander.'

'Who died,' said Merlin, 'in Babylon?'

'Ah,' said the old man, 'there hangs a tale worth telling. If an Alexander died in Babylon, it was not *the* Alexander. I am Alexander.'

'Bring him water to wash his hands,' said Arthur. 'Bring him food and drink – and then, Alexander, tell us your story.'

And this was the story told by the old man –

'I am,' he said, 'Unconquered Alexander. Every part of my body, save my back, is scarred by the weapons of those who could not defeat me, and none of my men were ever killed running away. I led my army, fighting, to the End of the World, to the edge of World Encircling Ocean, and there I sat down and wept because there were not more lands to conquer.

'And as there I sat, my face in my hands, I heard a voice call my name – "Alexander!" 'I looked, and saw a most beautiful woman, who stood holding the bridle of a white horse. She wore armour like a man – golden armour like

127

mine, but the plumes in her helmet were scarlet. An Amazon, the loveliest woman ever I saw, in all the lands I'd travelled.

'Behind her, at the edge of the sea, were others of her kind, men and women, all beautiful, all dressed in golden armour, all sitting on the backs of white horses, or standing at their heads.

'"Alexander," said this lovely woman, "this is the end of your world, but there are other worlds. Come with me, Alexander. Are you brave enough to come with me?"

'My enemies have called me cruel, unjust, vain, a tyrant – but not even my enemies have ever called me a coward. A horse was led forward for me, and so eagerly did I reach for its bridle that I almost forgot my army. Only when I was mounted did I remember them, but when I looked for them not a sign could I see of my hundreds of men, my mules and horses, my elephants, my tame tigers, my wagons and catapults and siege towers.

'"They are hidden from you," said the lady, "as we are hidden from them. But you may go back to them if you wish."

'I did not wish – but still the thought of my lands and my cities troubled me.

'"We'll send one in your place," said the lady, and she beckoned, and from among her people came one who was more like me than my own reflection in a mirror. He walked away from the sea and vanished through a shaking of the air. "And now," said the lady, "you are free to come with me."

'And if, as you tell me, Alexander died in Babylon, then it was he who died, that man from another world, and not the true Alexander. He sits here, and drinks to your health.'

'I thank you,' said Arthur. 'But what happened when you followed the lady to her world?'

'I mounted my horse,' said Alexander, 'and rode at the head of that lovely company, beside their beautiful leader, over the very waves of the sea! The white horse left hoofprints in the white foam that topped the waves.

'It was soon dark, and for many hours we rode, with nothing to see but silver stars above and white foam beneath, and nothing to hear but the shaking of the bridles and the roll of the water.

'But at last the darkness lightened to a twilight, and through the smell of salt came the scent of land and flowers. Ahead we saw a shore – a place of flickering white waves, high cliffs and trees. Our company rode from the sea to the beach, and from the beach to the good land, and we trotted through pleasant shade of green woods where white deer ran from us.

'So I was brought to the army I was to command, which was camped on a wide, flat plain beside a red river. I looked about and saw many fine, tall, beautiful people, but also men and women with dog's faces, centaurs, headless people with eyes and mouths in their chests, and people with six arms or two heads. But I found them no less brave than the beauties.

'And so I led this army to war. I studied the maps and led them across rivers; I picked the ground, I led the charge; I laid siege to fortresses, and I never lost. And all this took three long hard years of campaigning – '

And Arthur, listening, nodded; Arthur knew –

'– and though I saw many strange sights and spoke with many strange creatures – yet I missed this world more and more.

'For in that world of theirs, Arthur, there is no full day and no full night – only everlasting twilight; and there are no mountains and no valleys – only an endless flatness. Nor is there savour in their food, or pleasure in their company, beautiful though they be. And, when the war was won, I said to the Queen, "Lady, now I must go back to my world – and the changeling you put in my place, you must recall him."

'She said to me, "He was recalled, long ago."

'"The more reason," I said, "for me to go back. Armies cannot go unled, lands cannot go unruled."

'"Here is a land to rule," she said. "Here is an army to lead. Stay here, and rule with me."

'Not a day, not an hour longer did I wish to spend in that land now that the war was won, but I would not offend the lady, and so I said, "Gladly I would rule here with you – but why should I not rule in this world and my own? I must go back to Earth. I'm ruler of many lands there, and I must take some care for their people. I must know if my friends are safe and well. And, Lady, I'm homesick for darkness and daylight, for mountainsides and deep, cool valleys."

'"Alexander," she said, "how long have you been here, in my world?"

130

'"Three years, Lady," I said. "Three years would be my guess, and that's too long to leave my rule to others."

'"It's been longer," she said. "You cannot go back."

'"I?" said I. "Cannot?"

'"Your empire, your cities, your friends . . . All have passed away, Alexander."

'"Then," I said, "I must go and win them back."

'She looked into my face and said, "You will never believe until you see for yourself." From about her neck she lifted a chain of gold, so fine and supple, it was like a golden ribbon, and she hung it about my neck and kissed me. "Go back. I'll give you a horse. It'll carry you over the sea to Earth again, and, when you have seen for yourself, it will bring you back here to me. But never take this chain from your neck until you return to me again – not even to wash, not even to sleep. Will you promise me this?"

'And I promised, thinking that once I was in my own world again, I would never wish to return to hers – but I would keep the gold chain as proof that I was a conqueror in two worlds.

'"In the word of Alexander I trust," she said, and then gave me presents – soft travelling clothes of fine wool, this sword, dagger and armour; and a bag, holding food, that would never be empty, and a flask full of wine that would never be dry. A white horse was brought for me, and a troop of cavalry escorted me to the coast and out over the sea, but left me and turned back long before I reached Earth.

'So I came back into our beautiful world, riding

my white horse and following the seagulls and the scent of flowers and leaves. I came back to the heat of our sun, which dazzled my eyes and drew the sweat from my skin, made my throat dry and my head ache, and it was glorious! I came back to our darkness and the cold of our night, the thick night scents and night dews – which is more beautiful, night or day? But no sign I found of my army.

'That white horse could gallop over sea waves, and move over land faster than a bird through the sky. I rode it through all the lands I had led my army; I saw all the mountains and valleys I had longed for. And I saw, everywhere, such small people – and great temples brought to ruin – and great cities emptied. Everywhere people stared and pointed as I rode by, but nowhere did I find spoken any language I had known.

'"Where is Alexander?" I asked. "Where is the army?"

'They ran from me and hid, and I rode on, and on, and came into my own land. Here, I thought, I should hear my own language spoken: here I should hear news of my friends. But the people I spoke to gaped at me, gaped at my clothes, at the brooch holding my cloak. They looked in my face and grinned, turned aside to their mates, spoke what I couldn't understand, and laughed at me – at me!

'I came to my father's city, to his palace, and the burying ground of his fathers. It was a mound, nothing more, its grass baked yellow under the sun. All about was a hot silence, and high above a hawk flew.

'I rode around the mound and came on some

shepherds. When I spoke to them, they understood me no better than all the others I had asked for news, but I dismounted and shared my food and drink with them and, after a time, we began to understand each other better.

'The old city? What, the one that had once been here, Alexander's city, the great Alexander? This was it – and the old shepherd put his hand on a hot stone that stood clear of the grass. It made you dizzy to think, he said, that the great Alexander had once ridden out from this heap of stones to conquer the earth, and had never come back – but that had been a thousand years ago.

'"A thousand years?" I said.

'Why, aye, they said. A thousand years. More!

'"A thousand years," I said.

'Why man, they said, you've gone white. Maybe not so long as a thousand years, if it takes you like that. What do we know? they said. We're only shepherds, we can only count to twenty. We've heard said, a thousand years, but it's not right, most likely. A long, long time ago, certainly, but not a thousand years. Time out of mind, before our great-great-grandads were born – aye, before Rome had been heard of, before Christ, even, when men like Alexander had been fathered by gods. But not a thousand years, that wasn't to be credited.

'But I had heard, and I looked at the ruins of my father's city standing against the hot sky, and I knew it had been a thousand years. I thanked the shepherds for their kindness, and I mounted my horse, and I rode on, to the north.

'To have the whole world to ride over, knowing that everywhere is strange and that everywhere are strangers . . . Often I touched the golden chain about my neck, and thought of turning the horse and riding over the sea to the other world. But I sickened at the thought of that dull, flat, twilit land. I rode further north. I crossed a stormy sea, and came here, to your cold, wet, foggy little country.'

'My rich, green kingdom,' said Arthur.

'Your wet, rich, cold, green land. And, three days ago, on a forest path, I came upon two of your small men struggling to lift a log into a cart. In my own time, I was called a small man, but never, then, did I see such little weaklings as I see everywhere now. I pitied them, and I stopped to help them. They dropped the log and ran from me when they saw me dismount, but I lifted the log myself and rolled it on to the cart bed . . . I felt a tug at my neck. The golden chain the Lady had given me – it had caught around a branch on the log and snapped. I felt it slide over my skin. It fell to the ground and shone beside my boot.

'The white horse threw up its head, turned and galloped away – it seemed to turn into mist and vanish, so quickly did it go. And I – when the chain snapped, I felt my spine sag, I felt age lean its weight on me. My flesh weighed heavy on my bones. Arthur – Arthur – until the chain broke, I wasn't like this.'

There were some in the feast-hall – some of the knights, some of the serving-men, who sniggered behind their hands and said, 'Old madman. Thinks he's Alexander, stringy old fool.'

But Arthur was the king who had pulled the sword from the stone, who had loved a witch and fought giants. Arthur had ridden into the Other World himself. He knew that the silver dazzle on the sea can hide more than water from our eyes. 'The stories say,' said Arthur, 'that Alexander was as beautiful as he was brave.'

Alexander hung his head. 'Unconquered Alexander is conquered by Age, by Ugliness, by Loneliness, a thousand years from home and friends. Once I gave a sack of gold to a soldier – now I must hope that I will be given a little to eat, a place to lie down and sleep. And hard, hard it comes to me.'

Arthur rose from his chair and himself refilled Alexander's cup. 'You are my wonder,' he said. 'Because you have come to my court, I can eat and drink without breaking my vow. Alexander, I am High King over all the kings of the Isles of Britain, but you were King of the World. You are welcome to my court. All I have is yours.'

And Alexander said, 'Thank you.'

But Arthur, Dragon of Britain, was a jealous king.

For many, many hundreds of years, Britain had been kept safe from invasion by the head of old King Bran, buried under the White Hill. But when Arthur heard of this, he dug up the poor old king – and why? Because Arthur couldn't bear that anybody but himself should have the glory of guarding Britain.

And what King – what king of any time or land – could happily share his court and his kingdom with Unconquered Alexander, even an Alexander grown old? Arthur honoured Alexander, but the more he saw him, the more he feared him, and the more he feared him, the more he hated him.

Alexander's armour was taken from him, and his sword and dagger. Many gifts of clothes he was given, but never his armour back. And never was he given a horse, for fear he might ride away. Guards were set to watch him – and the guards changed every day, so they could never become his friends.

So much Alexander had lost – his kingdoms, his youth, his beauty and strength – and now he was left little to do but sit all day, a sad old man, under the eyes of his guards. But the older Alexander looked, the more people whispered of how beautiful he had been; the longer he sat by the fire, dozing, the more people told stories of marches he had led and battles he had fought; the more gifts Arthur gave him, the more was heard of Alexander's wonderful generosity – for if the sea-foam had been silver and the leaves of Autumn gold, Alexander would have given it all away.

And the more these stories of Alexander were told, the more Arthur feared him. Arthur felt like a candle, whose light is lost in the Sun's light – and the candle wanted to blow out the Sun. Arthur sent for Merlin.

'Rid me of Alexander,' he said.

'Alexander's a sturdy old man yet, for all his thousand and thirty years,' said Merlin. 'Make up a hunting party, give him a horse and ask him to hunt with you. He's bored, he'll go. Then lead him, as if to hunt, to the wooded valley west of here. Lose him in the valley – and

I promise, he shan't return to trouble you.'

So Arthur sent servants to Alexander, with a horse, a hunting spear, a bow and a quiver of arrows; and he invited him to go hunting. Alexander was too old to run, but he eagerly hobbled to the hunt's meeting; he was too old to spear-leap to his horse's back, but gladly he put his foot in Gawaine's hands and was thrown up. Out with the hunt he went. With the hunt he went into the wooded valley.

And there the huntsmen – who knew the woods – drew their horses away from his. White mist curled around the trees and through the branches, growing thicker, hiding the horses and men – it was Merlin's mist. Soon Alexander was alone in a forest he couldn't see – he couldn't see a twig or a leaf, but only white mist. Nothing could he hear; the mist swallowed all sound.

Arthur, and the other huntsmen, came out of the forest in ones and twos. On the hillside above the valley stood Merlin. He held his staff in front of him and leaned his brow on it, and was so deep in the making of his magic that he was like a stone grown with lichen. The fog he had made rose out of the trees and covered the valley, hiding it from sight, until it seemed there was no valley, but, instead, the surface of a wide lake. It was so like a lake that a skein of geese, seeing it from above, came twisting down through the air to swim on it – and Merlin's magic was so strong that it held them up like deep water. But the geese didn't stay for long. There was no food for them there. It was a fishless, birdless, lifeless lake that hid the valley.

And under the lake, in the hidden forest, was Alexander.

When the mist had hidden everything from him, Alexander had dismounted and stood by his horse's head. He had called out to his hunting friends, but heard nothing but the boom of his own voice in the fog.

When the fog cleared, Alexander mounted again and walked his horse through the trees. He saw deer, but no men. He called, but got no answer – except for the boom of birds' wings as they rushed upwards from trees.

He tried to find his way out of the valley, but every path he followed turned back on itself and brought him again and again to the same place – where a little, fast-running brown brook threw itself into a deep pool grown round with ferns. The clearing was loud with the noise of water and rich with the smell of it.

Even when he left the paths and tried to find a way through the trees and briars, he came, after much walking and struggle, back to where the brook fell noisily into the pool.

This was Merlin's spell: that Alexander should never be able to find his way out of the hidden valley. Against Merlin's power, not even the great Alexander could fight.

The last years of Alexander's long life were spent under Merlin's lake, in the hidden forest. There, he who had led an army across the world, wandered round and round a small forest pool. He who had lived in the stone palaces of Babylon, built himself a small shelter of branches. For company he had his horse, the fish in the pool, the deer who came to drink at the brook, and the birds. All but his horse were afraid of him.

Because of the mist that covered the valley, there was no day or night for Alexander, but only a never-changing twilight, as there had been in the Other World. Day after day, sitting in his shelter by the brook, he would remember his friends, and his battles, the triumphal parades – but though he remembered so fiercely that he heard the sounds again, smelt the smells – still his friends were a thousand years dead, and he was lost in this forest he couldn't leave. Remembering only made it harder to bear.

'I am Alexander,' he said to his horse. 'I was King of Macedon and Great King of Persia. In Egypt, I was a god.' The horse tossed its head, not caring a jot.

When Alexander died, no one was with him, no one knew. So powerful was Merlin that the valley stayed hidden beneath the lake of mist for a hundred years after Merlin was shut in the oak. And when the spell faded and the valley was seen again – well, by then, all trace of Alexander, every bone and hair of him, had gone.

Better he had never left this world to go with the Lady; better he had accepted his fate and died at Babylon.

Or, having left this world, he should never have returned. He should have stayed in that flat-as-a-chessboard world with its endless half-light, and ruled there: ever-young and unconquered, for ever.

'And do you want Alexander's fate for me?' asked the head. 'Do you want me to live, lonely, beyond my time, only to tell you stories?'

The old woman and the children sat listening,

with tears in their eyes. They wanted so much to keep Linnet with them. Such fierce, choking pain was in their chests that, surely, their hearts were cracking into pieces.

'We will bury you,' said the old woman. 'Beneath the hearthstone. I promise.' And she wept.

The head sighed, and its lids fell heavily down over its eyes, for the last time. It never spoke again.

The old woman pried up her hearthstone that very night, and dug a hole beneath it, with the children's help. They kissed the head goodbye, and wrapped it again in its old shirt, and buried it, and replaced the hearthstone on its grave. Often, after that, as they sat by the fire, eating or talking, they would rap on the hearthstone and say, 'You hear that, Linnet? How are you?'

And the children grew up in good health, and the old woman lived to see them beyond the age of needing her, which was all she had wanted – so, surely, Linnet kept luck in the house, as he had promised. And, indeed, the house still stands, if you know where to look for it, crammed from wall to wall and floor to ceiling with luck, and by that hearth are always told good stories.